The rock-hard wetness of her heavy leather shoes had frozen her toes and blistered her heels. But now her feet were cozy inside the soft moccasins. She felt guilty about the others, still suffering, and then, astonished, saw that all the prisoners were being given moccasins.

She and Eben Nims stared at each other.

"*They knew* they would take this many prisoners, Eben," whispered Mercy. "They have enough moccasins to go around. They have little pairs and big pairs."

She thought of them back in Canada, around their fires, among their French allies, planning how many pairs of moccasins they would need when they sacked Deerfield.

They mean us to live, thought Mercy. But why? What will they do with all of us?

ALSO AVAILABLE IN DELL LAUREL-LEAF BOOKS

THE
RANSOM
of
MERCY
CARTER

Caroline B. Cooney

Published by
Dell Laurel-Leaf
an imprint of
Random House Children's Books
a division of Random House, Inc.
1540 Broadway
New York, New York 10036

Visit us on the Web! www.randomhouse.com/teens

Educators and librarians, for a variety of teaching tools, visit us at
www.randomhouse.com/teachers

ISBN: 0-440-22775-5

RL: 5.2

Reprinted by arrangement with Delacorte Press

Printed in the United States of America

November 2002

10 9 8 7 6 5

OPM

for Louisa, Brian and Liz

YEAR: 1704

PLACE: Deerfield, Massachusetts, the most remote settlement on the frontier

PEOPLE: The English (settlers are not yet called Americans), who live in New England

The French, who live in Canada

The Indians, mostly Mohawk, also in Canada

ATMOSPHERE: War. France and England are at war across the Atlantic Ocean, so the colonies go to war in the New World. The Indians fight on the side of the French.

AT STAKE: Money. The fur trade makes men rich.

Land. Left as wilderness? Or turned into farms?

Who will pay the price?

The children of Deerfield

Chapter One

D*ear Lord,* prayed Mercy Carter, *do not let us be murdered in our beds tonight.*

Mercy tucked her brothers in, packing them close. *Or any night,* she told the Lord, shifting her weight from foot to foot. Even though she wore both pairs of stockings to bed, the cold of the floor came through the heavy wool. It was the coldest night she could remember during a winter when every night had been colder than it ought to be. Downstairs, where the fire was blazing, one of the soldiers had tried to write a letter to Boston and his ink had frozen.

She kissed each brother good night. The boys were wearing most of their clothes, which made them fat and funny under the quilts. She dreaded getting into her own bed, because she slept alone, and only body heat could keep anyone warm tonight.

Before she shuttered and barred the window, Mercy

knelt to look out. In spite of twenty soldiers quartered in the village and every Deerfield man armed and at the ready, Mercy could never fall asleep until she herself checked the horizon.

Just below the window was the vegetable garden, covered now in three feet of snow. Against the barn, which sheltered one cow, two sheep and a pig, were drifts taller than Mercy, crusted over from freezing rain. Out beyond the stockade, icy fields gleamed like lakes in the starlight.

None of the children had been allowed out of the stockade since October. This winter a hen in the yard was not safe from an arrow, or a child from a bullet. Surrounded by thousands of square miles of wilderness—and they were 4 trapped in ten crowded acres.

Aunt Mary and Uncle Nathaniel and their two children, too afraid of Indian attack to stay on their farm, had been sleeping on the floor downstairs since the governor had first warned of possible attacks.

Four rooms. Seventeen people. Week after frigid week.

It was amazing that the three hundred citizens of Deerfield were not killing each other instead of waiting for the Indians to do it.

Lord, she wished her father were home. He had ridden down to Springfield to buy molasses and tobacco. Without Father, the house felt weak and open, even with soldiers sleeping downstairs. Even with Uncle Nathaniel.

Indians sneak up, Mercy reminded herself. Nobody can sneak across such crusty ice. We'd hear their feet crunching a mile away. Father said so.

Except that when the Indians had come last October, there'd been no sound. Mercy had been the only witness, leaning out this very window.

October in Massachusetts was crimson berries and orange pumpkins, tawny grass and bright red sumac. The colors called to Mercy like bugles; like battle cries. She had unpinned her hair to let the wind catch it and pretended to be the figurehead of a ship, although she had never seen the sea, or even a lake.

"I will lift up mine eyes unto the hills!" she told the horizon. She loved this psalm. *"From whence cometh my help."*

Swinging so far out the window that her fingertips barely held her safe, Mercy had spotted Zeb and John heading toward Frary's Bridge to bring in the cows. The tall grass around their thighs made them swim in dusty gold. Mercy's hair was the same color, like wheat in the sun, and she was admiring her own thick yellow hair when out of the grass appeared Indians, as natural as wildflowers. Before Mercy could choke back her psalm, they had encircled Zeb and John.

One shot was fired, one dash stopped, two surrenders made.

Zeb and John and the Indians vanished over a rise and out of Deerfield forever.

The boys had known better than to fight. Fighting meant a tomahawk to the head. Surrender meant a chance to live.

And Mercy had known better than to sound the alarm. Taking the boys was bait. The English would do anything to save one another. All the Indians needed to do was capture one white and the rest of the English would come running to the rescue.

Ambush was the Indian form of battle. They did not like casualties. It was not their plan that they should die; only whites. So if Mercy were to scream, the sentries would mount up and the whole village rush in pursuit. But the English would find their horses shot from beneath them, and where only Zeb and John had been lost, now twenty might die.

So Mercy had stayed silent.

The grass closed in, the captives were gone, and the world went on, full of color and glory.

I will lift up mine eyes unto the hills, from whence cometh my help? Mercy thought. Maybe in Israel, in the days of King David, the Lord sent help from the hills. But Massachusetts? Help does not come from our hills, Lord. Only Indians.

Mercy had shaken her fist at the Lord. *How could you let those savages take Zeb and John? Why aren't You on our side? You sent us here! Take care of us!*

4

Five months ago, and Mercy still trembled when she remembered her rage at the Lord God. It was the kind of thing that turned the Lord against Deerfield. Every sermon Mr. Williams had given this winter dealt with sin. The Lord had no choice, said Mr. Williams. Deerfield must suffer. Mercy had done her part to anger the Lord and she knew it.

Mercy pulled the shutter across the window, fastened it with the wooden bar and climbed into her freezing bed to consider her sins.

She had woven five yards of cloth today, but the Lord would not care about that. He would care that she harbored evil thoughts toward all three brides in Deerfield.

She was envious of Sally, who had gotten a perfect husband in Benjamin Burt. Horrified by Eliza, who had married an Indian, even if Andrew was a Praying Indian. Sickened by Abigail, whose choice was a French fur trader twenty years older than she was. How could Abigail marry a Frenchman? The French were the enemy. The English were at war with the French!

Besides, Jacques had no teeth. If Mercy had to marry the enemy, she would not pick a toothless one.

Mercy was too young to think about marriage, but she thought about it all the time anyway. There were no good husband choices. She was related to everybody, or they were the wrong age, or she would have to be their third wife and take care of six stepchildren as she gave birth to her own first child, like Stepmama.

When Stepmama married Father, she'd been bright and saucy. Two years later, she was gaunt and beyond laughter.

Mercy had taken over the care of her four brothers and little sister. The boys were usually good, but three-year-old Marah taxed everybody's patience. Marah was lovable only when she was asleep. She didn't sleep much and she didn't sleep well.

Stepmama was too worried about her own new baby to help. The fierce winter made it almost impossible to keep the baby warm. Stepmama would not set her down, for fear the tiny body would freeze.

At least Marah and the new baby slept between Father and Stepmama, so at night Mercy had some relief. But half the time, Aunt Mary and Uncle Nathaniel would hand her the two cousins to take care of as well. Mercy liked Will and Little Mary, but as more and more children were added to her care, Mercy had to pray constantly for patience.

Forgive us our sins, Lord, she prayed. *Let spring come soon. Let the Indians stay in the north.*

Benny and John were already asleep. Sam, the oldest, was curled against Tommy, who was still trying to find a breathing space. Tommy poked his head out from under the covers. "Mercy, do you think they'll come tonight?" he whispered. Tommy was only five. He didn't really know who "they" were.

"No," said Mercy comfortingly. "Remember, Indians

have to come all the way from French Canada. Nobody would travel three hundred miles in a blizzard."

But she knew this to be untrue.

White settlers based their lives on outwitting weather. While the men were building thicker walls, the women were knitting thicker stockings. Indians, however, did not hide indoors. Their lives were based on entering the weather.

"How far is three hundred miles?" asked Tommy. He had rarely been beyond the stockade. Built of great slabs of tree trunks, sharpened to points at the top, the huge fence was fastened on the inside by horizontal beams. Along these, the night watch would walk uneasily in the brutal wind.

"Three hundred miles is too far for anybody, Tommy. Sleep tight."

"Are you sure?"

"I'm sure."

Trusting his big sister, Tommy tucked himself into the elbows and knees of his brothers and slept.

But Mercy was not sure. She didn't trust the soldiers. What did they care about Deerfield? Every week they wrote to their commander, saying, "Nothing is happening here, let us come home." She knew how cold the nights were; how easy to drift toward a door in the dark, slip inside to find a fire and a hot drink.

From the fields came a vicious ripping sound, like a huge sheet being torn into rags. Mercy jerked upright, straining to comprehend the night sounds. Voices? The sharpening of knives? The priming of guns?

"Just ice snapping on the river, Mercy," said Sam softly.

"I thought you were asleep."

"Tried," said Sam. "Failed."

Sam was a year older than Mercy and hated imprisonment even more. He was so bored. No horse to ride, no hills to climb, no fields to run across. Mercy knew her brother prayed the Lord would end this captivity even if it meant the attack actually coming.

She heard a crunching sound, and then another. I will not get up, she told herself. I will not check the horizon again. I will rest in the Lord.

THE CARTER children slept.

Families who dared not stay on their own farms slept on other people's floors.

Animals slept in barns.

Soldiers slept in rotation.

FINGERS GRABBED Mercy's hair, twisting the thick yellow braid and yanking it tight. Her neck stretched and she could get no air. The scalping knife would—

All too familiar with this nightmare, Mercy suffocated her scream and hugged herself hard to keep from making a noise. The worst thing was to wake anybody up. They had had enough false alarms.

Lord, let me be braver than this, she prayed.

Downstairs, one of the soldiers was doing something with the fire. She heard the friendly clink of iron tools against brick, the whooshing collapse of embers and the rasp of a heavy log shifting.

Did she also hear movement beyond the shutter, or was that just the soft breathing of her brothers?

She slid out of bed and felt her way to the window. Her fingers found the familiar bar and as silently as possible she slid it back. When the shutter opened, the blast of air sucked the warmth out of her. Her nightcap had come off in bed, and cold rushed into her head, chilling all thought.

Mercy didn't like to think about heads because that made her think of scalping.

People could live through it. Mary Wells had. She still had her face, but there was no back to it. The edges of her face had tightened around the bone. Nobody had married Mary Wells and nobody would. Who wanted to wake up in bed with a skull on the pillow next to him?

A shawl hung on a peg by the window. Mercy held the fringed edge of wool over her mouth to warm the air.

The snow writhed with movement. It looked like the river in spring, schools of fish leaping in the lap of the water. Mercy could not imagine what she was seeing. There wasn't enough light to make out the shapes—and

9

then suddenly there was an immense amount of light and everything was clear.

The Indians had come.

Hundreds of them.

But Indians did not mass armies, like whites. They traveled in small bands. How could there be so many? They were leaping over the stockade! Impossible. It was twelve feet high.

Mercy saw what she should have seen yesterday, and the day before. Snow had drifted up and frozen solid. The huge fence was no longer a blockade, but a bridge.

She heard the long slow familiar creak of the stockade gate. No Englishman would open the gate. The Indians who had climbed over the stockade must have run through the village and opened the gates from the inside.

She realized why she could see. The Indians had fired the barns.

What fools we are, thought Mercy. We store our hay and kindling leaning against the barns. One flick of the torch and the deed is done. If we are not shot or scalped, we will be burned.

Mercy came to her senses. She slammed the thick wooden shutter, throwing the bar just as a bullet flew through the air. It thudded into the shutter, splintering the wood below her hand and half emerging into the room.

All Deerfield had awakened at the same moment and to the same horror. Three hundred people screamed together.

Mercy had listened to single shots all her life: killing a crow here, slaughtering a cow there. But a battle she had never heard. Now hundreds of guns were going off.

Beneath her came the splintering smash of doors and window frames being burst through.

The Indians were inside the house.

Indians in the field, Indians in the woods—yes. Indians with arrows, with bullets—yes. But the attack was supposed to stay outside. She stood rooted to the floor.

Furniture was being upturned. Plates smashed. There were thuds, one solid thump after another.

Over the cries of the English came wolf howls so alien, so gruesome, Mercy felt them through her spine instead of her ears.

Sam was out of bed, yanking Benny and John and Tommy with him. "Put on shoes," said Sam roughly, shoving pairs toward the little ones. "Maybe they'll take us captive. We'll need our shoes on."

Mercy had been waiting for death, in which shoes were of little consequence. She was astonished that Sam could think of shoes. Well, if they needed shoes, they needed coats. She got her cloak and Tommy's jacket, but fear made her stupid and slow.

Their stepmother tottered in, moaning deep in her

chest. She was holding the baby, but just barely. Marah, pulling her comfort blanket along the floor, clung to Stepmama's nightdress. Stepmama's eyes were open so wide they seemed ready to come loose and fall out. "Sam! Mercy! We have to barricade ourselves up here."

There was no way to do that. The only furniture upstairs was her parents' bed. The children slept on rough wool bags stuffed with pine needles. They had neither chairs nor chests. There were no bedroom doors, only thick hanging curtains. Mercy slid past her brothers to take the baby before Stepmama dropped it head-first onto the floor.

The shooting downstairs stopped.

It was not silent, because the fighting went on outside, but there was a pause within.

The children were gasping for breath from the smoky air. Mercy assumed the house was on fire. Which would be worse? To go downstairs and be tomahawked or stay up here and be burned?

Stepmama's face turned inside out with terror, and she backed up, screaming and sobbing and tripping on Marah.

Standing on the stairs was an Indian.

MERCY HAD ALWAYS wanted to see war paint. Now she had her wish.

Black zigzags crossed his bare chest. Black stripes encircled his eyes and snaked over his shaved head to the single lock of hair braided in back. The braid had been tossed over his shoulder to hang in front, and the braid itself was hung with scalps. They were quite lovely, as if he collected horses' tails in many colors.

In his hand was a tomahawk, which turned out to be a smooth rock on a wooden handle. The stone was speckled with blood.

Mercy stood between her brothers and death. She had no idea what to do. Beg? Pray? Kick?

Stepmama backed into her own bedroom, pulling the curtain shut, as if cloth might save her and the baby from the Indians. Marah, abandoned, began crying in her most annoying whine.

The Indian's eyes traveled slowly, examining each of the four boys before he focused on the sobbing three-year-old. Mercy had time to walk between the tomahawk and her little sister. Kneeling beside Marah, she said, "Hush now. It's all right."

Marah didn't hush.

The Indian's hand, large and dark and covered with drawings, landed on Mercy's shoulder. His fingers closed tightly, and she obeyed the pressure and returned to her brothers. Tucking Marah under his arm like a sack of grain, the Indian pointed a finger at each child. "Go," he said in English, nodding at the stairs. "Go down."

Albany Indians who came from New York to trade in

Deerfield spoke a little English, and Andrew, the new husband of Eliza, spoke the same English as the rest of them, but English from a Canada Indian in war paint?

Mercy swept the boys ahead of her. John and Benny and Tommy were too little to wake up fast and so they were too confused and sleepy to cry or fight. Sam was organized and calm, checking stockings and shoes. The boys stumbled down the narrow steps while the Indian entered the bedroom. He wore heavy leggings, but the rest of his body, split in half by white and black paint, was bare. In this terrible cold, he had come without even a shirt?

It was true then, what Mr. Williams said. Indians were not human. No real person could endure such a thing.

Onto the bed quilt, he tossed their nighttime drinking cups, Benny's fishhooks and Mercy's sewing needles. He found Sam's knives and John's book of ABCs.

Mercy could not collect herself. She could not even form a prayer.

"Go," said the Indian. "Leave house." Eyes that did not seem like eyes stared at her from a face that did not look like a face. Mercy backed away from him and tried to go down the stairs, but the boys had come to a halt at the bottom.

Mercy looked over their heads. Hanging from the ceiling were hats, bullet pouches, strings of dried red peppers and apples, yarn in skeins and powder horns. Indian hands were plucking them down.

Mercy forced herself between her brothers and on

down the narrow steps until she could see what blocked the way.

Bodies.

Only last night, Mercy had cleaned that floor with sand, scrubbing on her knees, sweeping it down the cracks, until the floor was white. Now it was red.

In this warm familiar room where Father read every night from the Bible while Mercy knit, here the soldiers had bunked, and here they had died.

They looked as if they had been talking or smoking their pipes and been slaughtered where they stood. It did not look as if they had fought back. Perhaps they had never even bolted the door, expecting to come and go when it was their turn to walk the stockade.

She looked for Aunt Mary, Uncle Nathaniel and her two cousins, but they were not there dead or alive. Fire spread gaily from one soldier's pile of blankets to the next. The painted Indian bumped Mercy in the middle of her back.

"Step over the bodies," said Mercy to her brothers. "We must go outside. Here, Tommy, I'll help you." She sounded as if she were lifting him over mud on the way to church. Perhaps the Lord had answered her prayer and made her brave. He had certainly answered another prayer: they were going to leave the stockade.

Sam gave Benny a push and John a hand and then the Carter children were outside.

The burning village was spectacular. Flames lit the sky. Snow gleamed gold and orange. From one house came deafening gunfire, Deerfield men shooting out the upstairs windows and Indians shooting back.

The chaos was unimaginable. Painted and fearsome in the firelight, the attackers were red and white, black and white, black and red and white, slashed and zigzagged like lightning.

The fire spread, with its own horrific sound, sparkling as it devoured.

Hell will be like this, thought Mercy. All I love turned to ash.

And then a unit of French soldiers in scarlet jackets with gold braid appeared. They even wore their swords.

The presence of Canada French stunned her. For three hundred miles there were no roads; there were hardly even paths. They would have walked on frozen rivers; slept without shelter; eaten with their fingers. Just to get to Deerfield, this little button of a town in the middle of nowhere? How could Deerfield matter so much?

A bullet took a Frenchman in the chest and knocked him down at Mercy's feet. His companions surrounded him, exposing their backs to the Deerfield guns. Lifting the wounded man, they rushed him inside the Catlin house.

The Indians paid no attention to the wounding of a Frenchman. In fact, they paid no attention to anything.

As if nothing at all were happening, they lined their prisoners up. Mercy and Sam, Tommy and John and Benny stumbled into place, and now Mercy saw that the line was long. Dozens of children had been thrust out into the cold, where they stood stunned and silent. There were some parents.

She counted the entire Kellogg family. All six Hurst children. Some of the Williams children. Mercy found herself next to the oldest Williams girl, who tried twice to speak and twice could not; who pawed at Mercy's shawl and scrabbled at the fringe. What bodies had *she* had to step over to get out of her house?

Her father was the minister. Mercy loved Mr. Williams. He was the voice of God. Deerfield could not survive without him. Surely *he* could not be dead. "Your father and mother?" Mercy said finally.

"John and Jerusha," came the whisper.

John was six years old; Jerusha a newborn. If the Indians would kill John and Jerusha, they would kill Marah.

Mercy left her brothers, running back into her house, slipping in blood and ignoring flames. Her Indian was at the hearth, adding pots and spoons to his bundle. Stepmama was standing next to him, staring blankly, the baby asleep on her shoulder. The savage still held Marah upside-down under his arm and Marah was still holding her beloved blanket. Mercy remembered that she too was carrying things: Tommy's jacket, her own cloak.

Mercy walked in front of the Indian and said loudly, "I'll carry my sister," pointing to show what she meant.

His eyes rested on Mercy. Then he put his hand on her hair.

I'm dead, she thought. He'll scalp me right here.

But the Indian handed Marah over, and with both arms free, he tied his loot into a bundle, using the four corners of Mercy's blanket. He threw the sack over his back.

"Wait. I need a coat," said Mercy, reaching into the bundle and yanking out a warm covering for Marah. "Come, Mama," she said, but her stepmother did not move. "Walk on," said Mercy, shoving her. "Don't drop the baby."

Perhaps being upside-down had prevented Marah from whining, because as soon as Mercy got outside and turned her upright, she started shrieking again.

The line of prisoners had changed; it was moving; people were being forced out of the stockade and into the frozen fields. Her brothers and the Hurst children and the Williams children were gone and Mercy ended up next to Jemima Richards.

"They're going to kill us," cried Jemima, her body convulsed by sobbing.

"They had time to do that and they didn't," said Mercy. "I think we're prisoners." She forced Marah to stick her arms into the coat she had snatched, but it was Benny's and far too large for Marah. It would keep

18

Marah warm to her toes, but it meant Benny wasn't wearing anything. Where were the boys? She must catch up to them and button Tommy into his jacket. She looked around. She had already lost Stepmama and the baby.

There were too many people. She couldn't think straight about so many people who needed so many things. Jemima held on to Mercy so hard that Mercy could barely keep her grip on Marah. Burning barns fell in and the shrieking of penned animals filled the air. They had to get out of the stockade or burn. "Hurry, Jemmie. We have to catch up."

"I don't want to," moaned Jemima. "I'm English. This isn't fair. I don't want some savage near me. They even gave me a pack to carry. I don't want to carry it."

"Go!" said Mercy, jabbing her.

The north wind flung embers into the air, tossing them down to burn on, like candles in the snow. Mercy's family had never been able to afford candles, just pine knots.

"Where's my mother?" moaned Jemima.

"We'll find her," said Mercy. "Move faster, Jemima."

Ruth Catlin stumbled into line with them, wearing only her white nightdress. On her feet were huge heavy boots that must be her father's or brother's. In the reflected fire, Ruth's dark hair seemed to turn blue.

Ruth was frail and had bad lungs. Nobody had expected her to live through the winter. No young man spent time with Ruth because if there was one thing a

19

young man needed, it was a strong wife. Ruth didn't qualify.

She'll freeze to death quicker than I will, thought Mercy. She gave her scarf and cloak to Ruth, who snapped them through the air as if whipping a bare back. "Somebody let those savages in!" yelled Ruth, stamping her foot and whirling in circles to find the evidence. "There is a *traitor* here. Who opened those gates?"

Mercy had seen the attack. There was no traitor, only the stupidity of Deerfield, convinced that snow and cold were a barrier. She put Tommy's little jacket over her shoulders until she could find him. It was a beautiful thing, heavy boiled wool the color of charcoal, a gift from Boston relatives. It had no effect on the cold. Ruth took her time wrapping herself in Mercy's thick cozy cloak.

"I'm finding out who it was!" said Ruth. "I'm *killing* them."

As if there were not enough killing.

Out of the meetinghouse came a row of white men roped together, a crowd of women carrying babies, and older children carrying blankets and coats and little brothers and sisters. Dozens of prisoners. Had they fled to the safety of the meetinghouse only to find themselves trapped? Or had the Indians put their prisoners inside to keep them from being shot in the melee?

They were herded like cattle toward the gate.

Mercy made out her brothers far ahead, half hidden by smoke. She counted only three. *Oh, no! O Lord! Who's missing?*

They're all here, she told herself, I just can't see through the smoke.

The last pair of settlers out of the meetinghouse were Eliza Price and her Indian husband.

"I bet *he's* responsible!" said Ruth. "He's an Indian himself, for Lord's sake! She married him, which is disgusting. An English girl choosing an Indian?"

It was certainly amazing. But not only had Mr. Williams agreed to the marriage, he had performed it, and Eliza's family had taken Andrew Stevens into their home. Everybody said it was the only legal marriage in the New World between a white woman and a red man.

"He's a Praying Indian," Mercy reminded Ruth. It was as odd to have this conversation as it had been for Sam to think of shoes. Scraps of normality were flying around like burning embers.

"So Andrew claims to be Christian," snapped Ruth. "So he doesn't use the name Strong Arrow anymore. What makes everybody think the man suddenly became Weak Thread? I would never take a red Indian into my house. Andrew Stevens opened our gates. I know he did."

But if anyone had betrayed Deerfield, it could not have been Andrew.

21

Eliza was moved aside to make room. Then Andrew was hacked to death by his own people. Andrew did not fight. He stood still and erect while they chopped him to pieces and did not fall until he was dead. He seemed to have known it was coming. When it was finished, the Indians put Eliza in line next to Ruth, where she stood numbly, staring at her husband's body.

With the sharp edge of hatchets, the Indians prodded the line forward.

Nobody argued.

The huge gate had been half torn from its hinges. Captives were trying to fit through, trying to lead children, trying to count their families.

Mercy tripped on a little boy sucking his thumb and tugging sadly at his earlobe. He wore a frown and not much else. Mercy set Marah down and knelt in the shadow of the fallen gate to see who the naked child was. Little Daniel, his mother dead and his father away, left for the winter with his Warner cousins. His father had gone to Boston in the hope of finding a bride who would come to Deerfield and take care of Daniel for him. Boston women were too sensible to consider moving to Deerfield. In fact, there was not one Deerfield woman who would not have been joyful to move to Boston, but Boston had passed a law saying that to abandon a frontier town was the act of a traitor. If you lived in Deerfield, you could not leave.

Except now. They were leaving now.

Mercy hugged Daniel, who smiled around his thumb sucking and said without moving the thumb, "Hi, Merfy." Mercy wiped away Daniel's tears so they would not freeze to his skin.

"Where are the Warners?" said Jemima irritably.

Mercy did not want to know the answer to that. She had enough answers. "Daniel is our responsibility now, Jemima. Tuck him in your cloak while I carry Marah. And stop him from crying, Jemmie. They are killing the babies who cry."

Jemima would not pick Daniel up. He was too heavy, she said. Anyway, if she set her pack down, she would get scalped. "He's three," said Jemima, "he can walk."

Mercy took Tommy's jacket off her shoulders and bundled Daniel into it. She lifted the little boy on one hip and hoisted Marah on the other. Daniel settled in, putting one arm around Mercy's neck and still sucking his thumb. Even now, Marah did not want to share and tried to kick Daniel.

The sun was rising. It jumped out from behind the eastern ridge, throwing pink shadows over the snow and golden rays into Mercy's eyes. In minutes, the world went from dark to dawn to daylight.

There seemed no point in trying to catch up to her brothers, even if Mercy could have walked quickly with a child in each arm. Sam will take care of the boys, she told herself.

The snow had been so trampled inside Deerfield that

she had half forgotten it, but beyond the gate, the snow became a living creature: deep and solid, crusted and pathless. Leaders somewhere out of Mercy's sight were taking the line of prisoners northeast, and into the hills.

Only fifty yards beyond the gate, the weight of two toddlers already seemed impossible. Mercy was used to babies; most women in Deerfield had a baby every year. Not all of them lived, of course, but it took a lot of big sisters and cousins and neighbors to hold so many babies. Rocking them by the fireside was easier than carrying them uphill.

Mercy's breathing came hard. Jemima kept muttering and looking back while Ruth made threats from the safe warmth of Mercy's cloak and poor sad widowed Eliza stumbled.

Mercy paused to catch her breath and shift the children. She squinted into the rising sun, trying to make an accurate count of the prisoners, strung out now across a mile of snow. Smaller children were hard to see, hidden by snowdrifts or the long swinging cloaks of adults or being carried. When Mercy rubbed her eyes she realized it was not the glare of sun on snow that made it hard to see. It was tears.

She thought there might actually be a hundred captives. She had never heard of Indians taking more than one or two. There was no way to march a hundred prisoners, mostly little ones with short legs and hungry tummies, all the way to Canada in the middle of winter. No way to keep these children warm and their feet from freezing.

Already her feet, uncomfortably jammed into Mother's old leather shoes, were chafed and cold.

Cold replaced fear. She was not going to last long without a coat. *Lord, care for me. I have Marah and Daniel. I need to be strong.*

An Indian appeared next to her. He wore a deerskin cape and fat fur mittens. His black and white paint stared at her. It was not until he took off the cape and his chest was bare again that Mercy recognized him as the Indian on her stairs.

He put his cape over Mercy, tucking it around her and both the babies. It was lined with rabbit fur and had a hood, which he tied beneath her chin.

The Indian pointed Mercy forward and gave her a gentle push.

On this terrible morning, forward could have only one meaning: Canada.

Three hundred miles.

On foot.

In this weather.

Carrying two toddlers.

Chapter Two

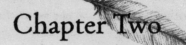

Deerfield, Massachusetts
February 29, 1704
Temperature 0 degrees

Eben Nims was last in the line of captives that straggled across the fields and up into the hills. The Indians had strapped a heavy pack to his back, its weight supported by a belt across his forehead. Wrapped in the quilt his grandmother had made in England were his mother's stew pot and china bowls, his sisters' dolls, his father's gun and his brother-in-law's Bible. There were boots and a whole ham, powder and shot and yesterday's bread.

Eben would not have to part with his family's possessions. He himself would carry them to Canada.

Next to him, Mercy Carter's stepmother could not even carry her own baby. Terrified beyond thought or action, she skittered aimlessly in the snow, mewling like the infant she held. Eben tried to take the baby for her, but so quickly that she could not have known what was happening, she and her baby were disposed of. Eben even understood why it was done. She would not have made it over the first mountain.

So these were the border wars, where the French sent their tame Indians to slaughter English settlers. The taking of so many children would strike horror into the heart of every frontier mother and father. Farms and villages would be abandoned. The settlements would return to wilderness. The New World would be French, and not English.

But in spite of shock and fear, Eben Nims rejoiced. He had saved his three little sisters: twins Molly and Mary, age five, hair of gold and eyes of blue, and Hittie, the picky, feisty seven-year-old Eben loved best.

By the time Eben had been awakened by gunfire, already the sleepers downstairs were trying to find and load weapons and trying to hold the heavy front door against the Indians, who were smashing the lock with their hatchets and throwing their weight against the hinges. Eben tore his little sisters from their bed, carrying all three in his arms and leaping down the steep stairs. He yanked up the trapdoor to the shallow cellar where food was stored and lowered the girls into the dark. "Are you coming too, Eben?" begged Molly, who was afraid of spiders.

"I'll be up here fighting. Stay quiet. Soon the attack will be over and I'll get you out." Eben slammed the trapdoor down and their terrified eyes vanished from his sight. He kicked bedrolls over the telltale cracks in the

27

floorboards and the Indians smashed through the front door and were inside the house.

Eben prepared to fight to the death. Help would come too late for him, but his little sisters would be found. The settlers had experience; they knew to check cellars.

Eben had no weapon but a frying pan, which he used as violently as the Indians used their tomahawks.

Frenchmen poured into the house. Eben was so astonished to see the French that the pan slipped from his grasp. The French did not do their own fighting. The whole point of Indian allies was to be sure that the Indians took all the risk.

Before he could launch his fists, an Indian thrust a knife into his chest. Eben gave his soul to the Lord, but when the blade had penetrated half an inch, the Indian used it to prod Eben out of the house. Eben willed Molly and Mary and Hittie to stay silent until the men of neighboring towns spotted fire in the northern sky and came to the rescue.

Running two fingers through his own dark red greasepaint, the Indian marked Eben's forehead.

Why was Eben alive?

Had it been so crowded in the house that they did not know Eben had killed one of them? Or did they know well, and did this mark him out for torture later?

MERCY PULLED HER SISTER along while she carried Daniel, and then she carried Marah and hauled Daniel.

Jemima did not help. Ruth, whose lungs got worse in cold weather, was wheezing.

Mercy knew the hill they were climbing; it was the view from her bedroom window. Long since stripped of trees, because the settlers needed so much wood for building and for fires, the hills around Deerfield had no covering now but grass. To get trees big enough to repair the stockade, the men had to venture three or four miles from the village. In wartime, it was too dangerous. The very trees they needed to cut down in order to build safety were the trees behind which the Indians lurked.

Mother had loved this hill. She used to run up, shooing the boys ahead of her, holding Mercy's hand, saying, "In a moment, Mercy, we'll see the Lord's land, the land He gave us, waiting for an English ax and an English hand."

Mother would throw back her head and laugh delightedly at the sight of wilderness stretching north ready to be tamed and used as the Lord meant it to be, instead of wasted on Indians.

"Look!" cried Jemima. "Mercy, turn around! The men of Hadley are coming! We'll be saved!"

Mercy did not want to slow down. The Indians were letting prisoners rest once they reached the top. But she did fling one glance over her shoulder, and sure enough, the flames in the sky must have alerted the watch in Hadley. From the south came men on horseback, dozens of them.

Jemima was laughing and hugging herself. "They'll kill those Indians," she said smugly. "They'll slaughter those French."

But Mercy knew too well that Indians were always ready for a second stand. Don't look, she told herself. It's better not to know.

She looked.

The ambush was ready; she could see it from where she stood. The men of Hadley might kill some Indians, but they themselves would soon be killed.

Mercy could jump up and down and scream a warning, but the rescuers would not see her against the glare. And if they did, they wouldn't recognize a warning; they'd ride faster to save her.

Mercy hoisted Daniel and Marah one on each hip, and climbed on, feet sideways in the snow to get a purchase on the slippery tilt. At the top of the hill, she set them down. Her knees were trembling and her ankles hurt from being skewed around. When she lowered her exhausted arms, she wanted to cry along with Marah.

Jemima and Ruth had halted to enjoy the rescue. Ruth was clapping, while Jemima waved her hat and scarf.

The French vanished over the snow and across the brook, in the opposite direction from the hill up which the prisoners floundered. A few Indians were gathering the last plunder when the men of Hadley galloped up. A great cheer rose from the Deerfielders still fighting. It was a stirring sound, as full of joy as a shouted *Amen!*

Jemima forgot her fear and Ruth forgot her anger and they too cheered.

Tears wet Mercy Carter's face as she watched. From the besieged houses, the surviving English poured out. There was no pause. The men of Hadley rode right past the stockade, while the men of Deerfield raced on foot after them, hoisting long dark flintlock muskets.

Don't go after the Indians! she prayed. Stay where you are.

But nothing would stop this pursuit; the English would hurl themselves against the enemy to get a hundred captives back.

Mercy held Marah and Daniel tight against her so they could not watch.

The Indians pulled back, coaxing the pursuit forward.

One Indian was shot down, body twisting and arms flailing, and another great cheer came from the English. Then the French exploded out of the trees and Indians stepped from a cleft in the ground.

Sunlight caught the snow and the world took on an odd pewtery shine and Ruth's brother, marked out by the persimmon-dyed cap Ruth had knit him last fall, was the first one killed in the meadow.

LAST TO REACH THE TOP of the hill, Eben supported the heavy burden by tucking his hands behind him, so he could straighten a little and look back.

The English flag blew in a light wind, as if it did not know or care that its sons and daughters had died.

Eben's house was burning.

In spite of its heavy covering of snow, the wood-shingled roof had caught fire. Fire was melting the snow, but snowmelt was not putting out the fire. A window fell in, cracked by heat, and flames leaped out. For a moment the flames were small and yellow, and then something caught; ammunition perhaps, or grease in the pan by the hearth.

Spires of orange and scarlet streaked from the house and smoke blackened the snow.

The men of Hadley died in the meadow and Eben Nims died in his heart.

Molly and Mary and Hittie would be silent forever now.

THE CAPTIVES HAD NOT RESTED five minutes when the Indians moved them on. The French did not join them, nor were they visible. Those glorious uniforms and startling swords might have been swallowed by the frozen river.

The prisoners went down the other side of the hill, and Deerfield vanished. They could neither see their home nor smell it burn, because the wind was blowing the other way and the smoke stayed behind. Ahead of them, snow sparkled rose and gold and the sun shone bright.

A few Indians walked first, trampling out a path, while the prisoners trudged in single file after them. There were about twenty adult men, tied at the wrists and elbows. Around their necks were leather collars with two leashes, one held by the Indian in front, the other by the Indian behind. About the same number of grown women walked alone, because the Indians weren't letting husbands walk with wives. The mothers were stunned and heartsick and, above all, slow.

It was frightening to see their fathers treated like dogs and their mothers without hope. The children kept to themselves.

Mercy's legs throbbed, Daniel got heavier and Marah would not stop crying.

Eliza walked fast enough but had to be guided in the right direction. She didn't say anything about what had happened to her husband, Andrew, and nobody else said anything either. In fact, nobody talked.

Jemima cried as much as Marah, wailing for the rescue that had failed.

Ruth's lungs were as noisy as the crunching of snow.

They crossed field after field, the Indians constantly demanding more speed. Mercy did not know why the Indians were in such a hurry. They had killed anybody who could chase them.

EBEN HAD FALLEN a number of times, and this time when he struggled to his feet, the huge pack on his back

33

had shifted and he could not balance himself. An Indian saw and came over to adjust the straps.

Eben had not thought he could tell one Indian from another, but he recognized the two-fingered smear in the man's red face paint. It was greasepaint. Eben could smell the rancid fat.

The sight of his house burning had turned him into a mere collection of muscle, a tool to carry and lift, a body that would make a good slave. He supposed that was the purpose of taking so many prisoners. Slavery. The mark on his forehead must be the mark of ownership.

He, Eben Nims, had ceased to be a free Englishman. He was Indian property.

A hundred paces ahead, Ruth Catlin turned and saw how close to Eben the Indian stood. She had been raging anyhow and when her brother was shot in the meadow her rage had intensified. "Kill him, Eb!" shouted Ruth Catlin. "Just kill him! They're all murderers."

Eben could hear Ruth and understand Ruth and even agree with Ruth. He was in a position to seize the hatchet. But there was no fight in him. He followed the Indian.

The pace was relentless. This was not a walk. It was a march. Like soldiers, they must take another step. They did not walk in rhythm. Nor was there a drum, like the one used to call the people to meeting. Instead, there was the shining edge of a sharp blade, which surpassed any drumbeat in its demands.

MERCY COULD NOT KEEP up the pace. Gradually the line passed her by, until she was walking with Eben Nims, and she must not fall farther behind than that, because the Indians behind Eben were the end of the line. Daniel held tight and sucked his thumb. But not only did Marah refuse to walk, she kept yelling that her feet were cold, and she wanted Stepmama, and she needed her mittens, and she was hungry.

Mercy could walk, though not fast enough, and she could carry, though not easily. But she could not supply food, warmth or Stepmama.

Mercy tried to believe that Stepmama was up ahead of her with the baby; that it was so crowded and chaotic Mercy could not spot her. But in her heart, she did not think Stepmama had left the stockade.

"The savage put food in my pack, Mercy," said Eben quietly. "If you slip your hand into the opening near my left shoulder, there's a loaf of bread on top."

They walked on, considering whether the Indians would tomahawk her for stealing Eben's own bread. Well, they'd shortly tomahawk Marah for whining, so Mercy might as well get on with it. She set the two children down, and Eben bent his knees so she could reach and Mercy fished around in the pack. She slid the loaf out. It was long and fat and crusty.

Her Indian was watching. Mercy looked straight at him while she ripped off a chunk for Marah. He did nothing. Mercy decided to give some to Jemima too, which would give her something to do besides whine. She would give bread to Eliza and hope food would break Eliza's grieving stupor.

Marah didn't take a single bite. She threw the bread across the snow. "I want Mama!" she said fiercely. She glared at Mercy, as if all this hiking and shivering were Mercy's fault.

Mercy could not abandon the bread out there in the snow. She was going to need that bread. It was all they had, and somehow Mercy had become responsible for Marah and Daniel and Ruth and Eliza and Jemima, and probably even for Eben. Mercy stepped off the trodden path to retrieve the crust, but her Indian stopped her, shaking his head.

On his face was no expression but the one painted in black. His arms were tattooed with snakes that curled their fangs when he tightened his muscles. How could he go half bare in this weather? she thought, and then remembered that she wore his rabbit-lined cloak.

Daniel, sitting happily on her hip, reached out from under the rabbit fur and patted the snake. The Indian tensed his upper arm to make the snake slither. Daniel giggled, so the Indian did it again, and it seemed to Mercy that he actually smiled at Daniel.

Then, blessedly, he took Marah for her.

One child she could manage. One child was nothing. Now she would not fall behind. "Help me get Daniel on my back, Ruth."

Ruth removed the Indian's cape and lifted Daniel. He dug his heels into her waist, got comfortable and began to suck his thumb once more. Ruth tucked the cape in and around them both, tying the hood. Invisible and toasty under the cape, Daniel gnawed on his bread. Little crumbs fell down Mercy's back. She was able to walk as fast as Eben now. They were still last in line, but not in danger.

Up ahead, several children were being carried by Indians. Little Eunice Williams, the minister's youngest daughter, was actually riding on an Indian's shoulders, enjoying this strange parade, because she had a comfortable seat and a fine view.

Mercy's spirits actually rose. The distant hills looked like piled quilts. Her favorite psalm came back to her in all its beauty and truth. *I will lift up mine eyes unto the hills, from whence cometh my help.*

Faith passed through Mercy like a drink of something sweet and warm.

A moment later her Indian came up from behind, passing her and heading toward the front.

He did not have Marah.

IT WAS AN HOUR before the Indians paused again, and then they stopped so abruptly that prisoners were tripping over each other.

It frightened Eben. What was going to happen?

What dread plan might the Indians have for their white prisoners now?

No Indian lifted a weapon. They stood motionless, looking west.

Eben watched for several moments before he was able to pick out distant figures coming toward them. It was not rescue. If those were English, the Indians would long ago have surrounded and attacked them.

Slowly, the shapes turned into men; men carrying burdens; men bent double under the weight, yet not staggering as Eben had. They looked as if they had killed and were carrying entire cows.

They were very close before Eben realized he was seeing warriors carrying their wounded. Each hurt man was rolled up into a package, swaddled like a baby in blankets and strapped to a warrior's back. These men were carrying, by their foreheads and on their spines, a weight equal to their own.

Eben was awestruck.

Dropping his own pack on the snow, Eben's Indian knelt beside one of the wounded men, unwrapping bandages to examine the wound. His profile against the snow was beautiful as an eagle or a hawk is beautiful.

BLESSED REST.

Mercy flopped onto the snow. Daniel danced around, just a three-year-old enjoying the pretty day. Mercy closed her eyes so she could not see his happiness. She knew Marah was in the hands of the Lord. It's my fault. I didn't keep her quiet, thought Mercy, and she wept into the snow and then, because she had had so little sleep and so much horror, because she had walked so far and carried so much, Mercy fell asleep.

Even in sleep, she felt the extraordinary cold. The sleep was intense and short and she woke to the odd sensation of somebody unlacing her shoes.

I fell asleep with my shoes on, thought Mercy. Mother is taking them off for me. Mother is going to tuck me in and say my prayers for me.

Sam and Benny and John and Tommy loved stories about Mother, and Mercy loved to tell them. When she knew she was dying, Mother had pleaded with her children. Don't forget me, she had said, her eyes filled with tears. I will wait for you in the Lord, but don't forget me.

I will never forget you, Mercy had promised, but soon the shape of her mother's smile and the scent of her mother's hair disappeared from memory. Mostly Mercy remembered Mother by the house. Mother had had plans. Glass windows were what she wanted most. A real table, not a trestle and a slab of wood that had to be taken down between meals to make room for other chores. "Soon," Father used to tell her, smiling. She was a scholar, having read the Bible through many times, and there was nothing she liked more than telling the rough-and-tumble stories of the Old Testament.

Mother didn't get tired the way Stepmama did. It was nothing for her to weave several yards of cloth in one day and also kill two chickens, make a stew for ten, bake bread, help a sick neighbor, write Bible verses with the boys and show Mercy how to knit the heel of a stocking. Mother could accomplish anything.

Except her sixth child. She had not lived through Marah's birth.

The chill penetrated. It could not be Mother untying her shoelaces. Mother had not been alive for three years. Mercy woke up.

Her Indian, killer of Marah, was taking off her shoes.

"No, no!" she said, horrified. "I have to have shoes," she explained, as if his English vocabulary went this far. "I can't go barefoot. Let me keep my shoes."

But he threw them out into the snow, where they skidded over the crusty surface and vanished beneath hemlock branches like two brown rabbits. On her feet he placed deerskin slippers, lined with fur like the cloak. They tied at the ankle, with tall flaps to keep her legs dry and warm. She ran a finger over intricate embroidery. She remembered Mother stitching pretty things; a white ruffle on Father's best shirt; a narrow row of lace around the pocket of Mercy's Sunday apron.

The Indian pulled her to her feet, brushing the snow and ice from her neck and face, and put Daniel back in her arms. Daniel's feet had been bare, but now he too wore Indian slippers—just the right size for his little feet.

The rock-hard wetness of her heavy leather shoes had frozen her toes and blistered her heels. But now her feet were cozy inside the soft moccasins. She felt guilty about the others, still suffering, and then, astonished, saw that all the prisoners were being given moccasins.

She and Eben Nims stared at each other.

"*They knew* they would take this many prisoners, Eben," whispered Mercy. "They have enough moccasins to go around. They have little pairs and big pairs."

She thought of them back in Canada, around their fires, among their French allies, planning how many pairs of moccasins they would need when they sacked Deerfield.

They mean us to live, thought Mercy. But why? What will they do with all of us?

EBEN'S MOCCASINS were lined with thick black fur. His boots were abandoned at the edge of the trail. Eben thought of Deerfield men getting this far in pursuit and finding a hundred pairs of shoes.

It made him feel slightly better about the odds of survival. People who brought enough shoes would also have considered how to feed their prisoners.

Three hundred miles with, he guessed, a hundred prisoners, two hundred Indians and—somewhere, not here—perhaps two hundred French. A stupefying number of people to feed.

Eben tried to convince himself that the Indians had provisions waiting somewhere. But who could move enough food for hundreds of people all the way from Canada to Massachusetts? And how could that food be stored in the wilderness? And if they planned to hunt down meat as they marched, they'd have to leave the prisoners to do it. And they'd have to find a lot of deer.

He studied his Indian, trying to find answers in that paint-smeared face.

But his Indian now carried the full weight of his wounded friend or brother. One gesture, and it was clear that Indian would carry Indian, while Eben would carry loot.

Eben opened up the blankets to combine his pack with the Indian's. At the sight of his mother's dresses, Eben thought he would begin screaming, but he controlled himself. He tucked in his little sister Molly's doll as gently as Molly had every night.

O Molly! he thought, willing himself not to collapse. Forgive my sin.

Sarah Hoyt, watching from several places up in the line, walked back to help, but Eben's Indian called, "No!" The syllable cut as sharply as a knife edge.

Puzzled, Sarah motioned that she carried very little and could take part of the load for Eben.

"No."

One of the Kellogg boys, guessing that heavy loads were for men and not girls, also tried to take some of Eben's pack, but again the Indian snapped out a no.

"I'm just going to carry the heavy things," Joseph Kellogg explained. "The brass kettles—"

The Indian's glare terrified them. Joseph stepped away, holding his hands up for peace.

"I think Eben has to carry everything that belongs to his Indian," said Sarah softly. "We belong to somebody else. Stand up, Eben. Joseph and I will get the pack on your back."

She and Joseph could hardly even lift the double pack, and as for the straps, they were just a jumble of leather. Eben felt Sarah trembling against him, trying to get it done right and quickly. When another Indian strode up, they cringed, but he simply fastened the pack securely.

Eben wasn't sure he could take one step, never mind get to Canada.

JOANNA KELLOGG, one of Joseph's sisters, was stumbling.

For Joanna, the world was blurred. Her eyes didn't focus the way other people's did. Leaves on trees were green blots against a blue sky. She couldn't recognize people until they were within a dozen paces. When an Indian brave took Joanna's hand, she had not seen her mother die and did not know this was the killer.

She was only ten, but her pack was nearly as large as

the ones grown men carried. Joanna did not complain or call out. She just walked more and more slowly.

Ruth Catlin lost her temper. She flung the pack she had been given into the snow. She grabbed Joanna by the shoulders and ripped off Joanna's pack, flinging that into the snow too. She hurled an iron frying pan across the snow and then a whole leg of lamb. Indian and captive alike were mesmerized.

"You savages!" Ruth screamed. "Don't you even think about hurting Joanna. She's too little! You are vicious and mean! I hate you!"

She dragged Joanna forward as if the two of them meant to reach Canada first, by God. "Go ahead and kill me!" she yelled, holding out her hair to be scalped. "I dare you!" She made a fist around her own hair, yanked it tight and waved the bristles in Indian faces. Nobody tomahawked Ruth.

She stomped past Indian after Indian, calling them names.

Ruth stormed right up to the front of the line, where the lead Indians were trampling out the path. She could go no farther. The Indians politely stepped back and gestured north, making it clear that Ruth was welcome to lead the way.

Ruth kicked wildly at one of the braves, but he stepped back and Ruth's burst of energy vanished.

She wanted to lie down on her own soft bed, bury her face in her pillow and weep for the family that had died around her. Even more, she wanted to kill an Indian. Or ten of them. But she had no weapon and as for softness, even the snow was not soft today.

Well, at least she would not give those Indians the satisfaction of seeing her cry.

Glaring, dragging poor Joanna, she marched on.

IN A DARK AND TWISTED GROVE of spruce, a place Eben would have avoided in summer at high noon, the Indians stopped for the night. If he had ever seen a place where an evil spirit would dwell, this was it.

He knelt to release the pack. His forehead was rubbed raw, and beneath his coat, he was blistered from hours of friction and weight. The stab wound in his chest seemed to have deepened and widened.

No food was given out. There was no shelter. The Indians did not even start a fire.

We have to have fire! thought Eben. We have to dry our blankets and warm our feet! They stole whole hams. Surely they'll let us have hot food.

Could the Indians be worried that woodsmoke would reveal where they were?

No, because three hundred people left a considerable trail. And that same trail was littered with bodies and shoes. Even an Englishman who had never been in the woods in his life could stroll after them by starlight.

Eben decided the Indians were neglecting to make a fire just to be mean.

He watched them cut spruce boughs for beds, and the scent of spruce surprised him. It was sweet and friendly in the dusk.

Slowly, unthreateningly, Sarah Hoyt got to her feet. She dusted off her skirts and removed a bag she had tied to her waistband. She circled from child to child, giving each a bite of corn bread or dried apple. She must have grabbed the bag before she was thrown out of her house.

The Indians did not interfere.

Sarah Hoyt dropped down between Eben and Mercy. She gave a scrap to little Daniel and a crust to Mercy. Two circles of dried apple were left for Eben. He wolfed them down before he thought to wonder if Sarah herself had eaten any.

"You were wonderful, Eben," she said quietly. "I was proud of you, carrying so much and not giving up, and being sure that Mercy had bread for Daniel."

He had not been wonderful, but he did not explain. What was the point? Sarah had dead of her own.

"My father's up front," Sarah said. "You know how they've tied the men for the night? They're staked on the ground like skins being cured. I think the temperature's below zero again. I think they'll freeze."

Eben was hurt that he was not being treated like a man.

WITH DUSK, the snow turned blue and black. The heavy spruce boughs held as much snow as the loft of a barn. In this dark hollow, nothing had melted.

We will freeze to death, thought Mercy. Why go to the trouble of carrying a hundred pairs of moccasins when they won't make a fire?

Her Indian knelt and, with his bare hands, scooped out a hole in a snowbank. She expected him to store his plunder in the cavity. He had to make a lot of hand motions before she understood that this was her shelter for the night.

Not a house, nor a bed, nor even a stable. A hole in the snow.

Mercy wanted to raise her head to the skies and howl like a dog. But she wanted to survive. There must be no more bodies along this terrible trail. "First, may I look for my brothers?" She held up four fingers.

"No," said the Indian, and motioned her into the cave, tucking Daniel in after her.

Mercy would have felt much better if she could have rested her eyes on Tommy and John and Sam and Benny.

From her hole she watched the others settle in for the night.

Eben's Indian collected the older boys: Eben, the oldest Kellogg boy, the two Sheldon boys and Joe Alexander, who was in his twenties but looked very young. They were pinioned to the ground a dozen yards from where Mercy was curled.

For Eben, however, his Indian made a cradle of spruce boughs. He wrapped a leather rope around Eben's wrists and linked the cord to his own. If Eben moved, his captor would know it.

The rest were made to lie on open snow. There was nothing between them and the weather. No walls, no roof, no parent.

Daniel slept.

Mercy needed to pray before she slept, but her weary mind could not locate a prayer.

The sounds of the night settled into the rhythm of breathing: people too exhausted to care where they lay. Mercy waited for stars, so she could count them, and it was a long time before she realized the forest was so deep that trees hid the sky.

Lord, she prayed finally, *don't go.*

And yet her dreams, when they came, were sun-gilt and sparkly, as if the day had been made of crystal instead of blood. In her dream, it was October, and the leaves were gold. She gave a leaf to Marah, and Marah smiled.

Mercy awoke sometime in the night to a whispery shuffle. No doubt an Indian guard prowling. How careful were his steps. How slow and separate.

If only it would snow. She and Daniel would be hidden in their tiny cave, forgotten while the Indians marched on, and after a while she would dig them out and they'd run all the way home.

But was there a home now?

Mercy caught the edges of her mind like a hem with a needle, turning under the memory of the attack and whipping up the frayed and bleeding edges. She must not think of Deerfield. She must not picture what was left, nor what Father would find when he got home.

Anyhow, she could not let her brothers go to Canada alone, so even if she got the chance to escape, she couldn't take it.

It occurred to Mercy that a guard would not tiptoe. Her heart soared. *One of the prisoners was escaping.*

A load of snow tumbled off a bough and when the limb lifted, a shaft of moonlight fell on Joe Alexander, who had been tied down next to Eben. He was creeping out of camp.

Mercy prayed Joe out of sight and across the frozen ravines, prayed him back up and over every hill, prayed him safely to Deerfield and then—

And then, thought Mercy, the Indians will kill somebody in revenge.

Eben, probably. He was closest. They'll know that he knew.

Chapter Three

The New England wilderness
March 1, 1704
Temperature 10 degrees

Somebody was tapping Mercy in the ribs. It couldn't be Tommy, who pounced, or Sam, who jabbed. It wasn't John, who kissed, or Benny, who snuggled. Whichever brother it was had wet the bed in the night, and wet Mercy with him, and so far it was still warm, but the moment she separated from that sleeping brother, it would be cold and awful.

But the tapping would not stop, and Mercy woke to see a deerskin legging with a painted running deer. "Up," said her Indian. The paint had partly peeled off his face, giving him a patchy smeared look.

She remembered the day before backward: the marching, the carrying, the slipping, the snow. She thrust memory away, folding it closed. She would not think about the attack.

Lord, please, she prayed. *Let me see Sam and John and Tommy and Benny. Let Uncle Nathaniel and Aunt Mary and the cousins be*

here. Let it not be true about Marah. Let Stepmama and the baby be
safe and sound and walking fast enough.

The Indian stooped to take her hand and pull her to
her feet, giving a slight grunt as he did. For the first time
she saw that he too had been hurt and that the paint on
his side was his own dried blood, and Mercy knew then
that she had experienced war, and that it was true about
Marah. She did not take his hand, knowing what it had
done. Rolling Daniel ahead of her, she was out of the
snow hole and on her feet in a moment.

There was some sort of assembly going on. The prisoners were stumbling toward Mr. Williams, who stood
alone, his hands raised to the sky.

How extraordinary, thought Mercy. They're going to
let us pray.

She was glad, because a day without morning prayer
was unthinkable, but it didn't seem like something the
Indians would permit. French Indians were Catholic,
though, converted by priests from France itself. Mr.
Williams often said that if you were Catholic, you hated
God and were evil and stole little children from their
beds.

The warriors had gathered in clumps. Yesterday had
been complete victory for the Indians, and yet there was
no rejoicing among them. Her captor's eyes were on a
bundle in the snow. She had seen enough death in her
life to know it. One of the Indian wounded had not survived the night.

The posture of her Indian was human. It was grief.

"Mercy, I'm hungry," said Daniel, and she said, "Hush. We'll eat later."

Mercy was hungry too. The hunger wasn't yet pain, because Mr. Williams often called for a fast and Mercy was used to going twenty-four hours without food. No matter what woe was visited upon Deerfield—shaking fever, crop failure, the snatching of Zeb and John—fasting made Mercy feel safe again. If three hundred people ate nothing for a day and a night, surely the Lord would be impressed and might relent, and people would get well and corn would grow.

She and Daniel took a moment to squat behind trees. They cleaned themselves with snow, and when she washed his face with a handful of icy white powder, Daniel giggled. He wanted to wash Mercy's face too, and she let him.

By the time they reached the rest of the prisoners, Mr. Williams had begun speaking. He had a great deep voice that sounded just right when he read the prophets in the Bible. He could be Elijah, he could be Jeremiah. Mercy loved his voice. It was shaking now, but not with the ecstasy of belief that possessed Mr. Williams during a sermon. It was shaking with fear.

If the Lord is not with Mr. Williams, thought Mercy, the Lord is not with any of us.

She threw away a lifetime of training, and instead of listening harder to Mr. Williams, she stopped listening at all. Her prayer went so deep it had no form, it was just *Lord, Lord, Lord.*

And the Lord was good, for among the crowd, she saw Sam, John and Benny, her uncle Nathaniel, her aunt Mary, and far away from the rest, and separated from each other, her cousins Will and Little Mary.

She could not see Stepmama, the baby or Tommy, but no doubt they, like Mercy, had been separated. As soon as prayers were over, she would find them.

At some point during the night or early this morning, the French had joined them. There were far more soldiers than she had realized. A hundred French. At least two hundred Indians. With another hundred or so English prisoners, Mercy was among more people than she had ever seen gathered in one place.

They were standing in distinct groups, divided by expanses of gleaming snow. The still-bright French; the heavily armed Indians; the shivering English.

"The frown of the Lord," said Mr. Williams, "is very great. This dread suffering is because we failed Him."

I failed Him, thought Mercy. I did not save Marah.

Mr. Williams prayed for the souls of the dead, listing name after name. Among those whose souls he entrusted to the Lord were her brother Tommy, her stepmother and the baby.

No, thought Mercy. I let them all die? Even Tommy? *Sleep tight*, she had said to him. And now he would.

If she had not wasted time giving her cloak to Ruth?

If she had not taken Eliza's hand when Eliza went blind with shock? If she had shoved Jemima out of her way? Could she have saved Tommy?

The Indian next to Mr. Williams interrupted him roughly. "We kill. You tell."

Mr. Williams ceased to pray. "Joe Alexander escaped last night," he said. "If anyone else tries to escape, they will burn the rest of us alive."

Burn alive? Burn innocent women and children because one young man flew from their grasp?

Her Indian stood some distance away amid the other warriors. He was now wearing a vivid blue cloth coat of European design. In one hand he held his French flintlock, and over his shoulder hung his bow and a full otter-skin quiver—actually, the entire dead otter, complete with face and feet. His coat hung open to show a belt around his waist, from which hung his tomahawk and scalping knife. His skin was not red after all, but the color of autumn. Burnished chestnut. His shaved head gleamed. He looked completely and utterly savage.

He might sorrow for a dead brother warrior, but grief would make him more likely to burn a captive, not less likely.

Mercy imagined kindling around her feet, a stake at her back, her flesh charring like a side of beef.

Beside her, Eben seemed almost to faint.

Mercy had the odd thought that she, an eleven-year-old girl, might be stronger than he, a seventeen-year-old boy.

The English were silent, entirely able to believe they might be burned.

The first person to move was Mercy's Indian. Sharply raising one hand, bringing the eyes of all upon him, he pointed to Mercy Carter.

She was frozen with horror.

His finger beckoned. There could be no mistake. The meaning was *come*.

There was no speech and no movement from a hundred captives and three hundred enemies. It was the French Mercy hated at that moment. How could they stand by and let other whites be burned alive?

She had no choice but to go to him. She set Daniel down. Perhaps they would spare Daniel. Perhaps only she was to be burned.

She forced herself to keep her chin up, her eyes steady and her steps even. How could she be afraid of going where her five-year-old brother had gone first? O Tommy, she thought, rest in the Lord. Perhaps you are with Mother now. Perhaps I will see you in a moment.

She did not want to die.

Her footsteps crunched on the snow.

Nobody spoke. Nobody moved.

The Indian handed Mercy a slab of cornmeal bread, and then beckoned to Daniel, who cried, "Oh, good, I'm so hungry!" and came running, his happy little face tilted in a smile at the Indian who fed him. "Mercy said we'd eat later," Daniel confided in the Indian.

The English trembled in their relief and the French laughed.

The Indian knelt beside Daniel, tossing aside Tommy's jacket and dressing Daniel in warm clean clothing from another child. Nobody in Deerfield owned many clothes, and if she permitted herself to think about it, Mercy would know whose trousers and shirt these were, but she did not want to think about what dead child did not need clothes, so she said to the Indian, "Who are you? What's your name?"

He understood. Putting the palm of his hand against his chest, he said, "Tannhahorens."

She could just barely separate the syllables. It sounded more like a duck quacking than a real word. "Tannhahorens," he said again, and she repeated it after him. She wondered what it meant. Indian names had to make a picture.

She smiled carefully at the man she had thought was going to burn her alive as an example and said, "I'll be right back, Tannhahorens." She took a few steps away, and when he did nothing, she ran to her family.

Her uncle swept her into his arms. How wonderful his scratchy beard felt! How strong and comforting his hug!

"My brave girl," he whispered, kissing her hair. "Mercy, they won't let me help you." In a voice as childish and puzzled as Daniel's, he added, "They won't let me help your aunt Mary, or Will and Little Mary either. I tried to help your brothers and got whipped for it."

He stammered: Uncle Nathaniel, whose reading choices from the Bible were always about war, and whose voice made every battle exciting. He needed her comfort as much as she needed his.

"Uncle Nathaniel," she said, "if I had done better, Tommy and Marah—"

"Hush," said her uncle. "The Lord set a task before you and you obeyed. Daniel is your task. Say your prayers as you march."

In a tight little pack behind Uncle Nathaniel stood her three living brothers. How small and cold they looked.

Sam lifted his chin to encourage his sister and said, "At least we're together. Do the best you can, Mercy. So will we." They stared at each other, the two closest in age, and Mercy thought how proud their mother would be of Sam.

"Mercy," cried her brother John, panicking, "you have to go! Go fast," he said urgently. "Your Indian is pointing at you."

Tannhahorens was watching her but not signaling.

He isn't angry, thought Mercy. I don't have to be afraid, but I do have to return. "Find out your Indian's name," she said to her brothers. "It helps. Call him by name." She took the time to hug and kiss each brother.

57

How narrow their little shoulders; how thin the cloth that must keep them from freezing.

She had to go before she wept. Indians did not care for crying. "Be strong, Uncle Nathaniel," she said, touching the strange collar around his neck.

"Don't tug it," he said wryly. "It's lined with porcupine quill tips. If I don't move at the right speed, the Indians give my leash a twitch and the needles jab my throat."

The boys laughed, pantomiming a hard jerk on the cord, and Mercy said, "You're all just as mean as you ever were!"

"And alive," said Sam. When they hugged once more, she felt a tremor in him, deep and horrified, but under control.

AGAIN SHE WAS toward the end of the line.

The pace was hard. They were heading northeast, with the goal, she assumed, of reaching the Connecticut River. It would be frozen solid, an actual road through the wilderness, but first they had to get there.

It was one thing to follow a well-worn cow path over a hill stripped of its trees. It was another thing entirely to cut through the forest. Beneath the snow, like snares for rabbits or pits for deer, were the crevices and jags of the earth. Cliffs tumbled to the side. Fallen trees from ancient storms were like jumbled masts of ships thrown in the path. Tangled vine and briar grabbed legs and snapped against faces.

The men who had refused to exchange their boots for Indian moccasins had to stop and wring the blood out of their stockings.

As the day wore on, and Daniel fell, and Mercy fell, and Ruth fell, and Jemima fell, and Eben fell; as each time they were slower to get up and saw yet another mountain ahead and understood that they were not going around, they were going over—well, Mercy did not know how long they could continue.

She was often overtaken by Indians coming up from the rear. Except for Tannhahorens, Mercy could not yet tell one from another. Were these the same two or three, circling and checking? Or Indians just now coming from the battle site? Or—more likely—returning from hunting the escaped prisoner?

Mercy found herself checking scalps. Joe Alexander's hair was curly and brown, pulled into a tail which itself curled and flopped. She found herself thinking, No, that one's too blond; that one's too short. By nightfall, horrifying as this pastime might be, she knew that nobody had caught Joe. He had gotten home.

Such as it was.

Mercy put one foot ahead of the other and refused to think of Deerfield.

Sarah Hoyt had been given some moose jerky by her

Indian and she passed chunks to the other children, who chewed as they walked. It was as hard and dry as a shingle on a roof.

Sarah's Indian had divided his loot, carrying his share tied in English blankets but putting Sarah's share inside an Indian leather sack. The forehead strap that attached Sarah's burden was embroidered with glittering glass beads. Every time Mercy looked at Sarah's headband, she wondered whose fingers had made that. Whose needle; whose design?

She always thought of Indians as being men; warriors. But the strap was proof that there were also Indian women. Women who loved beauty; who spent time on embroidery as once Mercy's mother had spent time on ruffles.

"Does it hurt to carry things by your forehead?" she asked Sarah.

"No. It's heavy, but it rides well. At least so far. By dinnertime, it'll probably bother me." Sarah was laughing. "If we have dinner. If we don't, I'll really be bothered."

Hairpins and bonnets had not been in Sarah's mind when she was yanked from her bed, so her beautiful auburn hair was not fastened up and hidden but streaming in the wind. Mercy marveled that nobody had scalped Sarah. Didn't the savages see that coppery red hair and want it?

Perhaps they did not scalp because of hair color.

How did they make their decisions? How did they decide who deserved life and who did not?

"How can you laugh about anything, Sarah?" said Jemima. She wiped tears away and sniffled heavily. "I hate this! I hate everybody. I'm not doing it."

"Then you'll be dead," said Mercy. She could not be patient with Jemima. They all carried burdens, in their hearts or in their arms.

"Jemima," said Sarah, more gently, "did you not listen to Mr. Williams? We have to survive for each other and for the Lord. It is our duty."

Jemima kept crying.

Mercy with Daniel and Sarah with her pack put their minds on their feet and walked faster. Behind them straggled Ruth, wheezing and carrying nothing; Eben, carrying everything; Eliza, barely carrying herself; half-blind Joanna, whose pack had been taken back by her Indian after Ruth threw it and who now carried only a fur rug draped over her shoulders, which made her probably the warmest prisoner on the march.

Jemima carried her pack in her arms, sobbing into it.

Joseph Kellogg, Joanna's brother, had three toddlers literally in tow, each child holding to a rope he'd wound around his wrist. It had been his plan that they would stumble less if they kept a grip on the rope. But to such little children it was a game. They skidded along, letting Joseph pull.

"Go, horsie!" cried Waitstill Warner. She was a pretty

little girl; cold but not aware of it; hungry, but forgetful of that too. Daniel wanted to get down so he could be hauled on the rope like his cousin Waitstill.

"They're having fun," Jemima accused. "It's wrong of Joseph to be making sport. Their mothers are dead."

"Jemima, Joseph is keeping them from crying," said Sarah. "They don't know how awful this is. They're having an adventure."

But Jemima would not be comforted.

"Here," said Mercy, "have some jerky. You'll feel better." She didn't really want to give it to Jemima. Jemima was perfectly sturdy. Anybody could fast for a day or two.

"I will not feel better," wept Jemima. "I want to go home. I want my mother."

There were plenty of mothers on the march, but not Jemima's. Jemima was one of the stranded children. No father or mother, no brother or sister. Whatever had happened to their families, nobody had seen it or nobody wanted to talk about it.

"I will be your mother," said Mercy, who was exactly the same age as Jemima. She had, however, been mother to her brothers for three years. "Now hush, Jem. We must not fall behind."

And then a creek, so fast-flowing that even in this wicked cold it had not frozen. The Indians stood in ice water up to their thighs, handing the small children across, but the adults had to wade. Wet clothing froze to the body. In this wind, at this temperature, that could spell death. Should you fall in and get entirely wet, could you even get back on your feet in the force of that current? Would not your heart stop and your lungs fill?

The adults dithered fearfully along the ice-rimmed rocks.

Lord, thought Mercy, wishing for solid English shoes instead of Indian slippers, I have to get myself over, I can't let Daniel fall in; Ruth needs help, she hasn't thrown anything today because she's so tired she can hardly put one foot in front of another. Joanna can't see and Eliza is still only half here.

When her turn came, however, the Indians lifted Daniel from her arms and passed him safely to the other side. Mercy took a deep breath, steeling herself to enter the frigid water, but Tannhahorens lifted her as if she weighed nothing and set her ashore, dry and safe. "Thank you, Tannhahorens," she said.

They handed Ruth over as well, but Ruth did not thank them. "How could you?" she said to Mercy as the march went on. "How could you thank that man for anything? *He killed your family.*"

As the day wore on, Mercy ceased to worry about Eliza, who seemed able to walk steadily even if she had lost speech and hearing. She ceased to worry about Jemima, who was just going to cry forever. Instead she

63

began to worry about Eben. It was not the pack on his back that was hurting Eben.

Sarah Hoyt, who was Eben's age, tried to comfort him. "Eben, do not despair." She talked softly, to avoid Ruth's notice. Ruth was not a comforting person.

Eben shrugged.

"We will get there," said Sarah. "Wherever it is, whatever it is, we will stay together and we will get there in the Lord."

"No," said Eben. "I have sinned."

They had all sinned and they were all paying for it. A mile later, Sarah said, "Tell me the sin."

"Pride. I was so proud of myself for saving my little sisters."

Eben's little sisters were beautiful. Mercy adored them.

Molly and Mary and Hittie hadn't left their house in months. Englishmen were not hunters. If they accidentally found deer or turkey, of course they shot it for dinner—or tried—but they were farmers, not sharpshooters. Indians, however, could hit anything, far away or close up. Mistress Nims was not about to let them pick off her daughters.

Mercy's restrictions had never been that harsh. Inside the stockade, at least she had been able to go from house to house, from barn to woodpile, and to meeting on Sunday.

Patiently, obediently, the little Nims girls stayed in,

week after week. Too little to weave, because they couldn't manage the loom, they could knit and they could sew. They were the only girls in Deerfield ever to stitch samplers. Nobody else had the time to do it or the mother to insist.

"What happened, Eben?" said Sarah.

"When I woke up, the attack had begun. My mother was downstairs screaming that the Indians were at the window. I put the girls in the cellar to keep them safe," he said to Sarah and Mercy. "But the Indians fired our house. My sisters burned alive."

"Oh, Eben," whispered Sarah. She took his hand and they walked on together. "You did not set the fire. Do not hold yourself guilty."

Poor Eben! thought Mercy. No wonder he believed the Indians when they threatened burning us alive. It happened to his sisters.

Mercy prayed that smoke had taken Molly and Mary and Hittie; that they never felt fire. The story affected her feet; she could not seem to walk as fast, nor find the energy to care.

"I want to go home," said Jemima. "How many days of this? I can't do it."

Mercy drew a deep breath. "Jemima, stop crying. They hate it when you cry. And we don't know how long it will take. But Sarah's right. We can do it."

Jemima stood staring blankly at a horizon endlessly replacing itself with more hills and more wilderness.

She had been crying for hours now and had given up wiping her nose. Her hair had gathered in filthy hanks and she stumbled blindly like Joanna.

They came to a snowy hillside as steep as a tilted plate, down which a hundred people had already slid or fallen. Older children slid down on their stomachs or backs. Eben wriggled out of his pack and gave it a shove downhill. It made a channel in the snow. Joseph's three toddlers let go of the rope and whooshed down, giggling.

"I'm a sled, I'm a sled!" shouted Daniel, tumbling down the hill and bumping into Sarah Hoyt's ankles. Sarah fell over and a dozen children piled on top of each other, laughing, and had to be sorted out and turned upright by Indians.

"Come, Eliza," said Eben, reaching for her hand, but she neither heard nor saw, so he put his arm around her waist and the two of them skidded down together. At the bottom, several boys started a snowball fight. Eben made snowballs for each side, handing them out as fast as they could be thrown.

"I can't go on," said Jemima dully. She let go of her pack.

Mercy forced herself to take Jemima's hand and pull her on. "You have to try, Jemmie. They will tomahawk you if you don't."

"I don't care."

"Of course you care." Mercy picked up Jemima's

pack. She could carry it in her arms, it wasn't that heavy. She'd still be able to lift Daniel when she got down to him. "I'll carry this for you, Jemmie. You carry yourself."

But Jemima did not move.

Mercy linked her arm through Jemima's to haul her forward, but Jemima would not or could not go.

They were the very last English at the top of the hill.

It was suddenly terrifying and eerie: children playing at the bottom as if this were recess from school; parents far off, on their leashes; and Mercy and Jemima, left behind.

Jemima's Indian appeared at their side.

He had been one of the braves carrying a wounded warrior, but his warrior had died that morning. All day he had walked apart, paying no heed to Jemima that Mercy had seen. He continued to carry the body. Mercy did not know if he planned to take it home to Canada to bury or if he could not yet bear to part with it.

Now, quite gently, he separated the two girls, taking Jemima's pack away from Mercy. "Carry boy," he said to Mercy, pointing down the hill at Daniel. "Go."

Mercy met the Indian's eyes. They both knew Jemima had told the truth. Jemima could not go on. And if everybody walked north and left her behind, what would happen? Jemima would be meat for predators.

So when the Indian said again, "Go," Mercy skidded down the hill, but she could not miss the cracking thud of stone against bone.

The tremor that had destroyed Jemima, partly destroyed Uncle Nathaniel and was quivering inside her brother Sam invaded Mercy's heart.

I will be brave, she told herself. I will stay strong.

Lord, Lord, Lord, she said to Him. She had never needed Him more, but in this cold white wilderness, she could not feel His presence.

The snowball fights ended.

The sledding stopped.

The march went on. Nobody could help Mercy. Everybody had their own trembling legs and hearts to deal with.

Tannhahorens appeared by her side. He had covered his ears and shaved head with a great scarlet muff of a hat. In his long blue coat, he was astonishing, like something out of a Bible story. With mittened hands, he lifted Daniel from Mercy's back, giving the little boy another bite of hard bread and setting him on his shoulders to ride high and comfortable, the way Eunice Williams was riding. Then he took Mercy's hand to keep her from falling as the march went up yet another hill.

Chapter Four

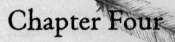

The Connecticut River
March 2, 1704
Temperature 10 degrees

Eben saw his sisters' smiles etched in the snow and their hair in the weeping branches of the willow. Yet he was not the captive possessed by rage. It was Ruth who stomped and fought and spat. When Joanna took the hand of her mother's killer, Ruth trembled with anger. "I won't forgive Joanna!" Ruth said in Eben's hearing. "She suffers from blurry eyes and maybe she didn't see it happen, but she's been told!"

Eben said nothing.

"I can't forgive Mercy either," said Ruth. "How could she just walk away and let them kill Jemima?"

Jemima's death already seemed remote. Six more captives had been killed since then. Eben hardly thought about them. To his shame, he thought about his stomach. They had had almost nothing to eat in three days.

When he was not thinking of his sisters, he was

remembering his mother's hasty pudding, how she would add hot milk and maple sugar. Her baked beans. How she mixed in molasses and chunks of ham to make the most wonderful dinner.

"And I will not forgive Joseph Kellogg for making a game of it," said Ruth.

Eben let Ruth yell. He didn't mind being yelled at, but the others had lost patience with Ruth.

The French had used Ruth's house to shelter their wounded during the battle. Ruth's mother had stepped across the bodies of her son and husband to nurse the bleeding French soldiers. Eben found this an act of Christian service beyond anything; maybe even beyond Christianity. Who could understand Mistress Catlin, saving the lives of those who had just killed her children? Minutes later, when Ruth was shoved out the front door and into the line of captives, her mother actually waved good-bye in the doorway, the only English settler left behind on purpose.

"Listen to Sarah Hoyt!" cried Ruth. Her long bony face was twisted with anger and hunger. "She's actually laughing. I despise her! It dishonors the dead to make friends with their murderers."

Eben's heart broke for Ruth. Was that how she believed her mother had behaved? Dishonoring her dead?

Ruth stormed over the snow to holler at Sarah, and Eben hoped Sarah would answer gently. But Ruth was caught by her Indian, who did not want the children's play interrupted. Ruth attempted suicide. She lunged at the Indian, grabbing his knife from his belt.

Eben ran forward, crying, "No! Ruth! No, she doesn't mean it!" he shouted to the Indians. "Don't—"

But her Indian simply caught Ruth's wrist in what must have been a painful grip and retrieved his knife.

Ruth was willing to hate her own as much as she hated the Indians. But the Indians did not accept her hate. They respected her. No matter what Ruth did, they thought more of her. They had even named Ruth, using a special word to call her. (She didn't come.) "Mahakemo," they called her, and they enjoyed saying the word. It just made Ruth madder.

It was amazing that Ruth would survive to kick and scream, she whose lungs had seemingly destined her for an early grave, while many who would be useful to the Indians, who would lift and carry and obey, were killed.

It came to Eben that the Indians were not deciding who deserved life. They were deciding who deserved captivity. Being the property of an Indian was an honor.

He just wished they were worthy of being fed.

THEY MARCHED.

"Ask your Indian his name," Mercy said softly to Eben. "They like that."

So Eben patted his chest and said, "Eben." Then he touched his Indian's arm and said, "Who are you?"

"Thorakwaneken."

Eben said it over and over until Thorakwaneken nodded and Eben supposed he had the pronunciation right.

Mercy pointed to a squirrel sitting on a branch. "Thorakwaneken," she said, "what is that?"

"*Arosen.*"

"*Arosen,*" repeated Mercy, and Eben echoed her. *Arosen.* Squirrel.

Eben would rather have had that knife pierce his chest and kill him than live to acquire an Indian vocabulary, but it was something to do and it kept Mercy cheerful. Eben did not much care if he lived, but he could not bear the thought of one more girl dying.

By nightfall, Eben and Mercy possessed a vocabulary of twenty-one words. They knew *redbird, sky, rock, spruce, knife* and the difference between *wood* and *woods.* They knew *fire* and *foot* and *hand.* So when Thorakwaneken took Eben's pack, gave him a light shove toward the forest and said in Mohawk, "Firewood," Eben realized he was being sent to gather kindling.

For the first time on the march, the Indians were going to permit a fire. The prisoners would be warm and have hot food.

"Go," said Thorakwaneken in English, and then in his own tongue.

Never had Eben been given an order he was so glad to obey. Moments later Joseph Kellogg was thrashing through the snow after him, breaking up fallen limbs and snapping off dead branches.

Eben envied Joseph, whose older brother, father and two sisters were on this march. How lucky Joseph was that his family had been largely spared. Of course, Joseph had not been allowed near his father or brother, his sister Rebecca was kept entirely separate by her Indian, and Joanna, whose eyesight was so bad, he was not allowed to help either. Still, Joseph did not have to imagine their final hour.

"Fire!" sang Joseph. "We're going to get warm!"

"We'll dry out our moccasins," agreed Eben, "and our pants and our blankets. We can warm our feet by the fire all night long."

"Do you think there will be food?" asked Joseph.

"No," said Eben. The French soldiers were gone, having moved ahead, fallen behind or taken another route. That still left three hundred to feed, and no Indian had gone hunting; they were too busy pushing their captives and carrying their wounded.

Eben chose a long heavy forked branch on which to stack his firewood and dragged the burden back to the camp, where he found much rejoicing. The Indians, it seemed, had paused here on their journey south from Canada to go hunting before the battle. Under the snow were stored the carcasses of twenty moose.

Twenty! Eben had to count them himself before he could believe it, and even then, he could not believe it.

Eben was no hunter. If he'd gotten one moose, it would have been pure luck. But for this war party to have killed *twenty*, dragged every huge carcass here so there would be feasting on the journey home—Eben was filled with respect as much as hunger.

The Indians made several bonfires and built spits to cook entire haunches. They chopped the frozen moose meat, and Thorakwaneken and Tannhahorens sharpened dozens of thin sticks and shoved small cubes of moose meat onto these skewers. The women and children were each handed a stick to cook.

The men were kept under watch, but at last their hands were freed and they too were allowed to eat.

The prisoners were too hungry to wait for the meat to cook through and wolfed it down half raw. They ripped off strips for the littlest ones, who ate like baby birds: open mouths turned up, bolting one morsel, calling loudly for the next.

When the captives had eaten until their stomachs ached, they dried stockings and moccasins and turned themselves in front of the flames, warming each side, while the Indians not on watch gathered around the largest bonfire, squatting to smoke their pipes and talk. The smell of their tobacco was rich and comforting. The wounded were put closest to the warmth, and hurt English found themselves sharing flames with hurt Mohawk and Abenaki and Huron.

One of the Sheldon boys had frozen his toes. His Indian came over to look but shook his head. There was nothing to be done. Ebenezer Sheldon could limp to

Canada or give up. "Guess I'll limp," said Ebenezer, grinning.

Thorakwaneken had taken four scalps. Nobody wanted to watch, but nobody could look away. With the flat of his knife, he scraped off the flesh from the underside until he had just skin and hair. He poked a row of holes along the edges of the skin. As calmly and carefully as Mercy would stitch a hem, he stretched the scalp and stitched it, loop by loop, to a hoop of willow wand. It looked as if someone had painted in a spider's web and hung a horse tail from it.

Every captive knew whose scalp had just been stretched but it seemed impossible; how could the farmer who had worn his brown hair long and tied in a double knot be part of the strange thing Thorakwaneken had just created?

The relief of warmth and food made the captives talkative. Until now the Indians had permitted little speech, but tonight their anxiety seemed gone. Mercy asked Tannhahorens if she and Sarah could sit with Eben and he nodded.

"You asked him in Indian!" said Sarah. "How did you learn?"

"I've learned some too," said Eben. "I like having something to think about besides—" He stopped. The golden yellow of the firelight looked like his sisters' hair.

"You did your best, Eben," Sarah said, and for a moment Eben thought Sarah was going to kiss him, but her kiss landed on the wind-chapped cheeks of sleeping Daniel, cuddled for the moment in her arms instead of Mercy's. They sat watching as the Indians bundled small children in layers of blankets and tucked them in a row, close to the fires.

"My theory," said Eben, "is that being a captive is an honor for the strong and the uncomplaining."

Sarah and Mercy considered this.

"Then why is Ruth alive? She complains all day long," said Sarah.

"But she isn't sobbing," Mercy pointed out, "and she isn't actually complaining. She's calling them names. She attacked her own Indian this afternoon, did you see? She was going to stab him with his own knife."

They giggled. It was scary to watch Ruth, and impossible not to. Instead of a blow to the head, though, Ruth was usually given food. It wasn't a method anybody else wanted to try.

"But Eliza doesn't fit your theory, Eben," said Mercy. "She hasn't spoken since they killed Andrew. If you let go her arm, she stops walking. Yet they're patient with her."

"I admit Eliza isn't brave," said Eben. "She's in a stupor. Maybe they respect her for caring about her husband so deeply."

Mercy had never liked thinking about Eliza marrying an Indian. But what was her own future now? Would she, would Sarah, would Ruth, end up marrying an Indian?

The image of Ruth Catlin agreeing to obey an Indian as her lawfully wedded husband made Mercy laugh.

"And they let Sally Burt live," Sarah went on, "and she's about to give birth right on the trail. They're letting her husband walk with her, and he's the only one they let do that."

Sally's courage was inspiring. Eight months pregnant, big as a horse, and she bounded along like a twelve-year-old boy. She had even taken part in the snowball fight. "I'm having this baby," she had said when Mercy complimented her. "It's my first baby, I know it's going to be a boy, I know he'll be strong and healthy, and I know I will be a good mother. That's that."

In Mercy's opinion, Sally Burt was holding her husband up and not the other way around. If she could be half as brave as Sally Burt, she would be satisfied.

At the crunch of footsteps they looked up, and then they stopped talking. Ruth was dangerous, not because of her habit of throwing things, but because every word she spoke was upsetting. They had begun to see that part of survival was staying calm, and Ruth could not be calm. Even the way she sat down next to them, flouncing her skirt and whipping her cloak, was angry.

Nobody asked what she was angry about now. She probably felt they shouldn't have eaten Indian meat.

Sarah chewed thoughtfully on the end of her skewer until she had shredded the wood like a tiny broom. Then she poked it in the snow and drew aimless patterns. "Suppose we do live. Suppose we do get to Canada. Then what?"

"I think we'll be slaves to the French," said Eben.

"The French are Catholic," said Ruth. "It's probably better to be dead."

"Then slaves to the Indians," he said, shrugging. "I'm already a slave to Thorakwaneken. I fetch his wood and cook his meat."

Sarah shook her head. "You're not going to be a slave, Eben. Your Indian likes talking to you. I think he may adopt you."

"That is disgusting!" said Ruth. "Adopted by a savage? Can you imagine living like this forever? Eating like animals, sleeping in snow caves, sharing your fire with your father's killer? We must pray for ransom." Ruth took her position as oldest and wisest. "Eben, never speak another syllable in that savage language. You and Mercy should be ashamed. How many dead did we leave in Deerfield? And you bounce alongside their murderers, saying, 'Tell me the word for "squirrel." ' "

Eben hung his head. Mercy's cheeks stained red.

"*Ransom,*" said Ruth. "That is the word you must cherish. An English word and an English hope."

Sometimes the governor of Massachusetts was allowed to pay the French to get a captive back. It took months or even years, with negotiators traveling back and forth, bearing gifts or making threats. Because of the war, Boston jails were full of French prisoners and sometimes those men were exchanged.

But it puzzled Eben that the Indians would make such an effort. Why walk all the way from Canada to Deerfield in this terrible season, suffer hunger, lose brothers, take the immense trouble to carry a hundred captives back to Montréal—just to sell them home again?

He decided not to say that he thought ransom was unlikely.

"Oh, stop it, Ruth!" said Mercy, outraged. "*You* are the one who is selfish. The Indians saw Eben kill one of their warriors. You remember the killing *you* saw. Well, they remember the killing *they* saw. Did you think the Indians were joking when they said they would burn somebody alive? Do you think they will pick somebody on a whim? They will choose *Eben*. Thorakwaneken must come to like Eben and we must help that happen. Eben must have *allies*, not more enemies."

Ruth's stabbing finger dropped to her lap.

Whether or not anybody was burned, the men still faced suffering: the gauntlet, a quicker form of torture in which a captive ran between two lines of Indians who clubbed and beat him. Anybody in the Indian village who had not gone to war participated in the gauntlet. It was their job to hit hard enough to avenge the dead. A captive might reach the end of the gauntlet and he might not. The Indians didn't care.

Eben wondered about his courage. Could he stay on his feet and endure the blows? Or would he be another Jemima and give up?

IN THE MORNING, they divided what was left of the meat—not much—and marched another mile. Every step, they could hear wolves howling, and Eben was afraid and also surprised. Wolves did not normally gather in packs as large as this must be. Nor did they usually howl so much by day.

The English bunched together, keeping close to the Indians. The Indians were armed, but would they protect their captives from wolves or just laugh if stragglers fell?

The mothers who were still alive (ten killed so far on the trail, by Eben's count, never mind the ones killed in Deerfield) were uniformly exhausted. They were used to labor every day of their lives. But they were not used to marching, and almost all had had babies recently. They lacked the strength for the grim pace and the Indians lacked interest in helping them.

If you were near your mother, or anybody else's mother, you had to be prepared to witness her death, and no one could ever be prepared for that. So the children avoided their mothers. Today, appalled by the new threat of wolves, mothers tried to summon their children, but the children did not come.

They burst out of thick woods to find what could only be the Connecticut River. Low banks edged a frozen expanse that formed a smooth road north.

Eben would have loved to farm here. Even hidden by snow, this was beautiful country; it was a sin for this land to lie vacant. God expected men to use their talents, not bury them, and He expected land to be used, not buried beneath trees. Every field of corn, every fence and gate, every ax against a tree: These turned wilderness into England.

Eben plotted the English town that would rise here, seeing property lines stretching down to the water, choosing the low hill on which a meetinghouse would be built.

At the river's edge waited another whole band of Indians, surrounded by yapping dogs and empty sledges. It had not been wolves howling at all, but sled dogs.

It was as amazing as the twenty frozen moose. The planning that had gone into this journey! Eben felt there must be some strategy here; some background to the attack on Deerfield that he could not yet understand.

If the attack had been meant to keep the English from taking more wilderness, surely the destruction of Deerfield was enough. But maybe not. Maybe the true horror for Massachusetts would be lost children. Maybe it was children the Indians wanted.

81

But then why bring all these adults?

Perhaps so the Indians could litter the path with bodies, like words on a page spelling, *Get out! Leave our land!*

Then why bother with moccasins and moose meat?

Had the Indians anticipated riches and wealth? And so the sleds were not for carrying children but for carrying gold and fine guns and silver plate? But nobody in Deerfield was rich. You went to the frontier because you were poor, not because you were rich. Surely the French would have known that.

"Munnonock," said Mercy's Indian.

Eben did not know the word or any of the syllables in it.

Mercy frowned, trying to work it out. She shook her head at Tannhahorens.

He pointed at her. "Munnonock," he said again. His voice lingered on the *m*'s and *n*'s, humming like a bee, and then, hand on his chest, he repeated his name, "Tannhahorens," and pointed at Mercy. "Munnonock."

Mercy had been given an Indian name.

Eben shivered. Names had power. It occurred to him that the real name of this eleven-year-old had a terrible power: Mercy. The Indians might show mercy to her and she, in turn, might show mercy to them.

Ruth said sharply, "Do not answer. You are English. Your name is Mercy Carter. Scorn him."

"Ruth, that isn't fair," said Sarah. "Tannhahorens owns her. She has to do as he says. Mercy, ignore Ruth."

Mercy had not even heard Ruth. She heard only the syllables meant to drag her, or tempt her, into another language and another life.

Munnonock.

EACH INDIAN SLED was made of curved wood, like a shallow, flat-bottomed spoon. Along the upper rims were lacing thongs. Strung out in front of the sleds were the eager straining teams of dogs.

For the most part, the wounded had died or were now walking on their own. Only a few had to be wrapped in furs and placed on sleds. The heaviest plunder was repacked and tied in with them: brass pots, iron pans, carpenters' tools and fine long guns.

The Indians decked a sled with their own furs and the stolen quilts of the English, and into the sled they tucked Eunice Williams, who was seven, a beautiful child with black hair and eyes and very rosy cheeks, and two golden-haired three-year-olds: Waitstill Warner and her cousin, Mercy's Daniel. Eunice was in charge and she had a wonderful time. They played I See This! and they played Count the Trees.

Waitstill could count, but it didn't mean anything to her yet, so she just called out any number. "Four!" she shouted several times, and Eunice would say, "Four! Good for you, Waitstill!"

Waitstill's mother had been killed on the march. Waitstill was too little to understand, and although she had asked often where Mother was, she was easy to distract.

The three children spilled out if the dogs took the curves too quickly or hit a rock beneath the snow, but they weren't very high up, so it was rolling over rather than falling off, and they just giggled while somebody ran to stop the dogs and rearrange the children.

There were also sledges with runners. These were heavier and could carry more without spilling. These were pulled by men.

English men.

The children had seen their fathers on leashes, tied and led. They had seen their fathers helpless to give them food, keep them warm or even keep them alive. Now they saw their fathers attached to traces, grunting and pulling like animals.

The mothers had no choice but to keep plodding. Rides on the sleds were never offered to them.

The children gathered around the Indians, clamoring for the privilege of riding. Everybody wanted a chance to be warm inside the furs and wave at the others and rest from the constant march. Running boys dashed alongside, bothering the dogs and trying to hang on to the end of the sled and be towed. After a while they played ball as they marched, using snowballs and calling out which trees up ahead were the goals.

Ebenezer Sheldon limped on. Frozen toes or not, Ebenezer never slowed down and never complained. He was the third English captive to be named, after Ruth and Mercy. His was an easy name to translate: Frozen Leg.

Eunice's Indian began teaching her to count in Mohawk, and by noon, Eunice Williams, yelling over the snow from her sled, could count from one to ten.

So could Mercy and Eben. So, in fact, could most of the children, shouting out the numbers as they pelted each other with snowballs.

Mercy wondered what Eunice's father was thinking about as Eunice began singing in Mohawk. The minister had not been made to pull a sledge, nor was he carrying a load. His Boston relatives were the most important ministers in all the New World: Increase and Cotton Mather. The Mathers would pay anything to get the Williams family back. Had the Indians known ahead of time who Mr. Williams was and what he was worth?

Mercy considered again Ruth's idea that there was a traitor. Had somebody sold out, telling the French and Indians in which house to find the minister? That his relatives had power and money?

More than one Indian seemed to believe he was the owner of Mr. Williams. There was a moment when Mercy thought they would divide the minister with a hatchet. But he still lived, and they let him lead prayer and, once, sing psalms.

Black and gray and brown cloaks and hats stretched ahead of her. She counted brothers: Sam and John and

Benny were up ahead, each with his own Indian, doing fine. She counted cousins: Will and Little Mary were managing. She counted the children on the sleigh: Eunice and Daniel and Waitstill.

Miles and miles they marched, past the barren silhouettes of chestnut, the straight poles of pine and the sagging arms of spruce. She could remember what had happened in Deerfield, and yet she could not remember. It seemed sealed off, like a folded letter fastened with wax.

"Can the Indians still be afraid of pursuit?" said Sarah Hoyt. "I can think of no other reason for such a desperate pace."

"Ice," said Eben briefly. "Spring is coming. If the river thaws, there's no easy path north. We'd have to work our way through the forest. And they have to be worried about food. I suppose it's better to stay hungry and cover many miles than stop to find food while an English army catches up."

Nobody wanted the English to catch up. Indian scouts at the rear would see the English long before the English saw them, and as usual, ambush would lead to yet more English death. And if the Indians were really pressed, they might melt into the wilderness and leave the captives to die alone, and that was the worst image of all.

"Look," said Eben. "The ice is broken by that creek. Let's get a drink."

Avoiding the soft ice, the captives knelt, cupping their hands to scoop up water. Indians carried little wooden cups attached by a thong to the waist and could drink with dignity, but the prisoners had to take one swallow at a time in their hands.

Eunice Williams stood up on her sled, a dangerous trick with the dogs racing and the sled jarred by every rut and ridge. She waved gaily. Her black hair swirled, her straight white teeth flashed an excited smile and her cheeks were red as berries.

To stop Eunice from risking a really rough fall, her Indian lifted her out and placed her on his shoulders to ride, putting Joanna Kellogg and Thankful Stebbins in the sled instead.

Eunice will be adopted, thought Mercy. The Indian will keep such a beautiful happy child for his daughter.

English women had babies all the time—six in this family; twelve in that. But Indian women hardly ever had more than one or two. And the smallpox that had ravaged Boston last year had probably done worse to the Indians; it always did.

So . . . were the Indians in need of children?

Perhaps the Indians came to Deerfield on a hunt for *children*, Mercy thought, just as they might come to the forest on a hunt for deer. Perhaps Mr. Williams means nothing. Perhaps it's Eunice who means something, and Daniel, and . . . me.

Mercy Carter. *Munnonock*.

It was warmer, and Mercy let her hood drop to her shoulders. When the sun struck her face, she repeated softly the Mohawk word for "sun."

"Oh, Eben!" breathed Mercy, thrilled and astonished. "Guess what?"

The glare off the ice was bothering him, and as the temperature rose, the snow on the frozen river was turning to slush. His moccasins were soaked and his feet were so cold he could hardly bear the pressure of each step. "What?"

"I can figure out Mohawk words, Eben!" she said excitedly. "*Sun* was one of the first words Tannhahorens taught us. And we learned to count, so I know the number *two*. *Thorakwaneken* means 'Two Suns.' Your master's name is Two Suns! And *cold*—that's the word we use most. Eunice's master is Cold Sun." She turned her own sunny smile on him.

Eben was unsettled by how proud she was. He did not want to compliment her. Uneasily, he said, "What does *Tannhahorens* mean?"

"I haven't figured that out. He's told me, but I can't piece together whatever he's saying. I don't know what *Munnonock* means either."

Mercy darted across the slush to her Indian master, and although they were too far away for Eben to hear, he knew she was asking Tannhahorens to explain again the meaning of his name and hers.

He knew, everyone on the frontier knew, how quickly

captive English children slid into being Indians, but he had not thought he would witness it in a week. He had thought it would be three-year-olds, like Daniel, or seven-year-olds, like Eunice.

But it was Mercy.

Ruth walked next to Eben. For once their horror was equal.

A mile or so of silence, and then Ruth spoke. "The Indians have a sacred leader. Their powwow. He has a ceremony by which all white blood is removed. They say it is a wondrous thing and never fails."

They walked on. The temperature had dropped again and each of Eben's moccasins was solid with ice. Every time he set his foot down, he stuck to the congealing slick of the river and had to tear himself free. Soon the moccasins would be destroyed and he would be barefoot.

"I know now why it never fails," said Ruth. "The children arrive at the ceremony ready to be Indian."

Chapter Five

**Leaving the Connecticut River
March 8, 1704
Temperature 40 degrees**

In the morning, the Indians split up.

A group of three warriors, their four prisoners, one sled and eight dogs vanished upriver. A few minutes later five warriors and two heavily laden captives crossed the Connecticut to go west along the icy path of a brook.

Mercy had thought that everyone from Deerfield would stay together; that somehow, far to the north, at the end of this journey, they would be Deerfield again, with the same brothers and cousins and neighbors, just colder.

How babyish. How stupid.

Already they were out of food again. The wounded and the youngest children had had two or three bites of goose that had been shot by the band of Indians at the river's edge. Everybody else had had nothing.

It was, after all, the end of winter. No food existed except meat. Flour could not be carried, bread could not be baked, berries and corn did not grow. It would be easier to hunt meat when small parties were scattered over different territories.

Mercy herself was so hungry, she was faint. Tannhahorens would despise her for it. She tried to keep her feet from weaving and her tears from falling, but she could not.

Tannhahorens took her hands and cupped them. Then he removed a small deerskin pouch from his belt and into her cupped hands poured dust. He licked his empty palm and lifted his chin at her to indicate that she was to do the same. Hesitantly, Mercy licked the dust.

It was parched corn, ground almost to the point of flour. It had a salty, burned taste. It surprised her, and she shuddered, but immediately she wanted more and took a second lick. It was good. It was even filling.

She glanced at the sky. The temperature was dropping. It would snow tonight. Three hundred people would have gone a dozen different routes, and by dawn, their tracks would be eaten by the snow, dusted by the wind.

By the time Mercy had sorted this out, her three brothers were gone. She panicked. "Sam!" she screamed. "John! Benny!" She ran from group to group, darting behind sledges, racing among the dogs, circling the fires. "Sam! John!"

What was the matter with her? How could she have stayed separate from them? Why had she not kicked Tannhahorens in the shins, as Ruth would have, and marched with her brothers no matter what he said? Ruth was right, he was nothing but an Indian!

O Father! she thought. O Mother! I let you down again. I didn't protect Tommy. I didn't save Marah or Stepmama or the baby. And now the boys are gone.

On her second screaming circle of the camp, Tannhahorens caught her. "Boys go," he said.

"But are they all right? I didn't say good-bye! You never let me talk to them at all! I don't even know their masters' names!" A new and even more horrifying thought struck Mercy. It tore the wind from her lungs and her voice broke. "Will my brothers and I go to the same place? Will I see them again?"

Poor Father, come home to find his entire family ripped away in a night. Father would comfort himself that Mercy was taking care of the boys—and he would be wrong.

Tannhahorens had fewer English words than Mercy had Mohawk. He could not understand this outpouring. He steered her back to his possessions. *"Raquette,"* he said.

Mercy jumped in front of him, blocking his path. He was hung with weapons in preparation for departure: knives, tomahawk, hatchet, gun, two bows, quiver of arrows. But something new hanging from Tannhahorens' chest gave her pause. A Catholic cross. Although in her whole life, Mercy had seen only one spoon and a belt buckle made of silver, she knew this cross to be silver.

She wrenched her eyes from its beauty. It would be a sin to find a cross beautiful. Religion must be heart and soul, not scraps of metal.

Tannhahorens pushed her along in front of him. *"Raquette,"* he said irritably.

"Raquette?" she begged. "Is that your town? Is that Sam's master's name? Are the boys together? Is Sam going to be able to watch out for John and Benny?"

This time, ragged trousers and a torn stained coat blocked Tannhahorens's way. The Indian looked harshly at the Englishman in front of him, and Mercy wished she had learned words like *please*. But Tannhahorens walked on and left them together.

"Oh, Uncle Nathaniel!" she said, and they wrapped their arms around each other.

He held her tightly. He had to clear his throat several times to find his voice. "Your brothers are not together," he said, "but they seemed all right. They were not afraid. Benny's Indian has a sled and he will ride as he did yesterday. John's with five other English, all adults. They will watch for him. And Sam is with the Kellogg girls. He'll be busy taking care of Joanna and Rebecca."

Her three brothers, going in three directions in the hands of strangers.

"They took my Will and my Mary in the last band," said her uncle. "I have some hope. The Indians treat my children tenderly. When nobody else had a morsel to eat, their masters fed them."

Sam. John. Benny. Will. Little Mary.

Gone.

In woods and ravines, among wolves and panthers, rattlesnakes and bears, the children she cared about most were alone. "And Aunt Mary?" said Mercy finally. "Where is she?"

There was a long pause before the answer. Long enough that Mercy knew what the answer must be.

"She slipped on the ice yesterday," said Uncle Nathaniel finally. "She didn't recover."

Yesterday I was happy, thought Mercy. I admired my new language. I enjoyed the sight of sleds on snow and great trees rising in the sky. I rejoiced in the Lord's world. But the Lord's world always includes suffering.

"Mercy," said her uncle, his voice shaking, "remember your English." He traced her features with his fingers, as if he must capture her image to carry with him, since he would have no son or daughter, no niece or nephew to carry. "Remember your mother and father. Remember your God. Remembering must be your first rule. *You must remember, Mercy.*"

In his eyes she saw a terrible fear, and she thought, He does not think he will ever see me again.

I do not think so either.

ONE CAPTIVE AFTER ANOTHER, they left, peeling away in relentless rhythm.

Sally Burt waved jauntily, as if she were still slim and agile, not soon to give birth.

Nine Indians, none of whom Mercy recognized, had no sled and would carry everything they had, including Daniel, their only prisoner. His pale hair shining, his strong chubby legs sticking out, Daniel perched in the embrace of some strange Indian as comfortably as he had in Mercy's arms. "Bye, Mercy!" he called, and put his thumb into his mouth and his head down on the shoulder of the savage.

O Daniel!

Not one of us goes with you. Whatever your life will be, you will have it with no mother, no father; no sister, brother, cousin or friend.

Lord, Lord, Lord.

Mercy stood waving long after Daniel had vanished into the piles of mountains, one after another, blue and shadowy. She felt Daniel had been swallowed by a sea dragon.

Deerfield will never recover, she thought. Lost children will destroy it as lost buildings and lost crops never could.

"Raquette," said Tannhahorens again, patiently. He produced a peculiar set of shoes. Slender sticks of pliable wood had been bent in an oval, tips overlapping and tied in the shape of a paddle. Woven through and around this wooden frame were sinews, making a sort of diamond-patterned sieve. Fastened to the center were bands of rawhide. After checking her moccasins and re-tying them, Tannhahorens slid Mercy's feet into the loops. She was standing on the sieve.

Tannhahorens put his own on and walked. A warrior with webbed feet. If she had not been heartsick, she would have laughed.

It took her a while to figure out how to lift her feet with such large contraptions stuck to them. But they were wondrous. Her feet no longer collapsed through the soft snow but stayed on top, leaving the most extraordinary prints behind her: a hundred lacy diamonds where each foot had come down.

Some windows in Deerfield had had diamond-paned glass. Mercy's mother used to say to Father, "Someday we will have windows like that."

Mercy put memory in the hands of the Lord and joined Eben, who was practicing on his *raquettes.* Ruth got none, probably because she would throw them away. Why waste them on her?

The trail wove through evergreens.

A dozen yards ahead of her, Tannhahorens moved gracefully over the folds of white. Although snow covered the floor of the world, making the wilderness appear trackless, the Indian seemed to be following a path he knew. As soon as the starry patterns of the snowshoes pressed down, the path was obvious and reasonable, and Mercy thought that if it had been summer, she too might have seen the path through the trees. As it was, she saw only the bright shaft of Tannhahorens's blue coat in front of her.

Twice the snow diamonds split. Up ahead, where she could not see it happening, their band was dividing and becoming smaller.

It had begun to snow again when the sled tracks turned west, and Mercy's group went north. Now Mercy was given a burden pack with a forehead strap, because they had no sled with them; her band would carry everything.

The country became brutal.

Slabs of granite rose in awesome cliffs of striped and craggy rock. At the bottom of ravines were vast rock piles where whole sides of mountains had fallen off. Spruce and hemlock grew so tightly together they were a wall of black. There were no colors in this wilderness. Snow poured out of the sky like milk from a pitcher.

What if she got lost in this terrible place? The snow would fill in behind her, and even an Indian would never find a missing child here.

The *raquettes* became painful. The backs of her legs cramped up and she had to stop and massage the kinks out. She took off her *raquettes* and slogged on in moccasins.

"Look!" called Joseph Kellogg.

Directly above, a dead pine rose like a spire. On its very tip sat an eagle, looking down with the majestic scorn of predators.

"Sowangen," the Indians told them.

Mercy repeated the new word to herself. *Sowangen.* Eagle.

The eagle took off with a muscular thrust, and a single feather swirled down, turning like the winged seed of a maple. Joseph flung away his pack, jumped over fallen branches and leaped upon a rock, reaching and stretching. The feather fell into his hands.

The Indians were joyful, as if the eagle had intentionally sent its feather to the English boy. "Sowangen," said Joseph's Indian, tapping Joseph's chest. Joseph too had a name now. Sowangen.

"Tell me your name," said Joseph.

"Aronhiowosen."

It means "Great Sky," Mercy thought.

The sky above truly was great—infinite snow falling over infinite wilderness. But the greatness of the Lord seemed diminished.

AT LAST they rested.

Tannhahorens sat, as Indians did, without a substitute for a chair. The English would look for a stump or stone

98

so they could sit up high. Indians preferred the ground, even when it was wet. He stroked his silver cross, as if comforted by its shape, although Mercy could not imagine Tannhahorens ever in need of comfort, and then he rested the cross against his lips.

She found herself wishing she possessed something that spoke of God; that she could have always with her, especially when God seemed to vanish as easily as small brothers and hope.

She sighed and then in shock saw for the first time just how tiny their band was. Five Indians. Six captives. Eben Nims, Sarah Hoyt, Joseph Kellogg, Ruth Catlin and Eliza, the widow of Andrew.

The Lord was truly against her.

Why do I have to be with Ruth? thought Mercy. She'll throw things and she won't do her share. And Eliza! She's still blind with grief over Andrew. You have to lead her. Joseph will go off hunting with his Indian and have a wonderful time. Eben and Sarah will fall in love and hold hands. I'll be stuck making sure Ruth doesn't attack anybody and Eliza doesn't fall off a cliff.

Mercy looked around to see if they were going to have anything to eat, and of course they weren't, so she couldn't even distract herself with food.

EBEN REALIZED that he need not worry about being burned or tortured. He was going to starve to death.

Eben had thought that up here, where nobody lived

or ever had, the deer would be standing in rows in the woods awaiting a bullet. He had expected rabbits and grouse, moose and beaver. But there was no game.

They built shelters from woven branches, piling spruce and hemlock on top to keep out the snow. Each day some of the Indians left to hunt and each day they came back with nothing. It had never occurred to Eben that an Indian could go hunting and find nothing.

He was not sure how far they still had to go to reach Canada.

He had seen a map once that showed the Connecticut River, how it split the colony of Connecticut in half, then cut up through Massachusetts, headed north through unknown lands and bumped into Canada. The northern part of the map was guesswork. Eben needed a French map, which would show the city of Montréal, where the French kept their government, and the St. Lawrence River, down which fortunes in fur were shipped. He could not ask his master. An Indian kept his map in his head.

The only good thing about this rough land was firewood. No human had ever gathered a fallen branch here. So they could stay warm, but they had nothing to cook over the flames.

It seemed to Eben the Indians ought to worry more about this than they did. They spent every daylight hour looking for game, found nothing and did not mention it. Instead, they sat by the fire, smoked and told war stories.

It was the captives who discussed food, describing meals they had had a month ago or hoped to have in the future. They discussed pancakes, maple syrup and butter. Stew and biscuits and apple pie.

Ruth said to Mercy, "You and Eben and Joseph are so proud of your savage vocabulary. Tell them they're Indians, they're supposed to know how to find deer."

"There aren't any deer," said Joseph.

Ruth snorted. "We just have stupid Indians."

Suddenly the whole thing seemed hilarious to Mercy: a little circle of starving white children, crouching in the snow, and a little circle of apparently not starving Indian men, sitting in the snow, all of them surrounded by hundreds of miles of trees, while Ruth spat fire. "Ruth," said Mercy, "do you know what your name means?"

"My name is Ruth."

"Your name is Mahakemo," Mercy told her. "And it means 'Fire Eats Her.'" Mercy began to laugh, and Joseph and Eben and Sarah laughed with her. Even Eliza looked interested, but Ruth, furious to find that the Indians were laughing at her instead of being respectful of her, began throwing things at Mercy.

Mercy rolled out of range while Ruth pelted her with Joseph's hat and Tannhahorens's mittens and then with snowballs; finding them too soft, Ruth grabbed her Indian's powder horn.

Mercy jumped up and ran away from Ruth and out into the snow, and in front of her were a pair of yellow eyes.

The eyes were level with Mercy's waist. They were not human eyes.

No deer for humans also meant no deer for wolves.

Mercy meant to scream, but Tannhahorens got there first, in the form of a bullet.

Wolf for dinner.

It turned out that the English could eat anything if they were hungry enough.

THEY MARCHED UNTIL THE CAPTIVES could not take another step. Eben dragged Eliza half the way and Sarah dragged her the rest. Mercy and Joseph took turns hauling Ruth. That night they slept like rocks, and in the morning Mercy understood why bears spent the whole winter sleeping. It sounded good to Mercy.

Perhaps it sounded good to the Indians too, because they did not leave camp. Instead, they built two fires, gathering an enormous woodpile.

Joseph was stripped of his English clothes. Too torn and filthy to bother with, they were tossed into the woods. He was given a long deerskin shirt and leggings that hung from thigh to ankle, held up by cords strung to a belt. Then came coat, hat and mittens, all Indian.

How dark Joseph's hair was. How tan his skin. Joseph looked like a young brave.

In a moment, the Indians did the same with Eben, whose coloring was very English, ruddy cheeks and straw-yellow hair. He did not look at all Indian, but in deerskin, he looked tough and strong and much older.

The girls were nervous. They did not want their clothes stripped off their bodies, no matter how torn and filthy. But Eben's Indian, Thorakwaneken, hoisted a flintlock musket and looked questioningly at each girl.

Mercy could not imagine what he was asking of her. Eliza did not notice him or the gun. And Ruth was the last person to whom a sensible Indian would hand a weapon.

Sarah, however, nodded. "I'm a good shot." She took the musket from Thorakwaneken.

Food was such a problem that even Joseph and Eben would be armed and sent forth to hunt. The girls would stay by the fire with enough wood to last for days, and Sarah to fend off wolves.

EBEN AND JOSEPH and their masters went south. Thorakwaneken had both gun and bow, but Great Sky planned to rely on bow and arrow.

Arrows could be shot in succession more quickly than a gun could be reloaded. And arrows were silent.

For Joseph, Great Sky had a small bow and arrow, yet another carefully considered supply brought from

Canada. Great Sky set the boy's hands in place to pull the bow and helped him nock the arrow on the taut sinew. Eben watched enviously. "Please?" he begged. "I can do it. I know I can."

He thought Thorakwaneken almost smiled and saw now that the Indian carried two bows on his shoulder. The one he had brought for Eben was a man's bow.

Joseph and Great Sky went one way, while Eben and Thorakwaneken walked another. It was an hour before Thorakwaneken stopped at a clearing. He had been hunting for an edge to the wilderness.

All that appeared was a rabbit, looking as tired and hungry as Eben. In another world, one small rabbit would mean nothing, but today it was meat.

With Thorakwaneken standing behind him, guiding, Eben drew the bow taut and aimed. It amazed Eben that the Indian would risk losing a meal by letting Eben try.

The rabbit struggled a little in a soft patch, Thorakwaneken nodded and Eben loosed the arrow. The rabbit was theirs.

Eben was so excited he wanted to dance and yell, but Thorakwaneken stopped him with a finger on his lips. In silence they retrieved the rabbit and Thorakwaneken let him carry it.

In the spring, thought Eben, I'll learn to canoe. Maybe trap beaver.

The French and Indian border wars were about beaver. Well, not in real France and real England; they were fighting about their kings and queens. But in the New World, it was fur. Who trapped it, who sold it, who made the profit.

France wanted to own every river and every beaver skin the Indians brought down that river, and they killed Englishmen who got close or greedy. Destroying Deerfield probably had more to do with fur than with children or ransom.

Now, if Eben had been out here with Englishmen—

Well, he never would have been. The English would get here tree by tree, using axes to remove the wilderness so they would never actually have to set foot in it.

If I were Indian . . . , thought Eben.

His hair prickled. The bow in his hand shocked him. *If I were Indian?*

Lord, he prayed, *take these thoughts from me.*

On the far rim of the clearing, they found deer tracks. Now the Indian shifted his gun. There would be no teaching here. This was survival.

An hour later, Eben understood why Thorakwaneken had brought him along.

It was on Eben's shoulders that the deer carcass was carried back to camp.

SARAH NEVER set the flintlock down.

Ruth sat as close to the fire as she could get, having armed herself with a clublike branch. Eliza they had moved close to the fire and were watching lest she get too hot or too cold.

105

Mercy had not let herself think about Deerfield. But today she could not escape her thoughts.

The image of her father alone in an empty house tortured her. He would wonder now about the value of the molasses and tobacco that had seemed so important to him when he left. He would have found Tommy's body, and Stepmama's, and the baby's. The burials would be over, and the minister from Hadley would have come to send their souls to God. Father would be sorting through their remaining possessions, although Mercy could think of none.

Mercy's grandmother had stitched a sampler when she was a girl in England: stiff pink roses climbing a bright green trellis. It had borders of interlocked keys and little squares of needle lace; an alphabet and a Bible verse. Philippians 4:8. It had been stretched on a frame of wood, and how Mercy's mother had cherished that sampler. It spoke of elegance and the Old World and the luxury of time. That sampler made it possible for Mother to believe that one day, yes, she would have windows with diamond panes.

Mercy knew Tannhahorens did not have the sampler. But other Indians had also been in the house and done their share of ransacking. She prayed the sampler was there for Father, because pinned to the back were locks of hair Mother had cut from her children's heads. Five locks: Sam, Mercy, John, Benny and Tommy. Mother had died before Marah's little head grew any hair.

Half the day passed before Sarah spoke. "It's my father's gun, you know," she said. She moved her thumb off the long shaft so Mercy could see the carved initials: *D.H.* for David Hoyt.

Mr. Hoyt had been one of the stunned adult captives; wounded, heartsick and stumbling. It was difficult to believe Mr. Hoyt would survive if his journey was like the one Mercy and Sarah were enduring.

"Are you scared of wolves?" asked Ruth.

"No. The men will be back by nightfall. I'm just glad to have my father's possession in my hands. I think I will never see him again, but now, in some way, I have his power, and I hope his blessing."

They sat in the silence of the grim woods. The sun went down fast and fiery, the fir trees jagged and black against the vanishing glow.

If Sarah would never see her father again, neither would Mercy see *her* father. Or brothers. Or neighbors. They were separated like ice floes on the river, some tumbling downstream, some caught on the rocks, while Mercy had to walk north.

There was no such thing as home now.

THEY LOST count of days.

Sarah said it was thirty, and Eben said it was thirty-one, while Ruth said it was a hundred. Maybe a thousand.

They walked now up a long slender lake.

It was the end of March or the beginning of April, the time of year when ice changed its mind whether to be ice or water. They were afraid of falling through. At least the Indians were walking first.

"It gladdens me to think that a Mohawk might tumble through the ice," said Ruth. "I've been praying. If the Lord is going to answer any prayer, surely he'll answer that. He'll send some Mohawk to a freezing death, his lungs filling with slush, the ice sealing over as he tries to claw—"

"Ruth," said Eben, "be quiet."

RUTH STORMED AWAY.

She hated the Indians and prayed constantly not to hate her fellow captives as well. They were becoming Indian lovers. Only the stupefied Eliza had avoided it— and that was because she loved Indians so much she had married one. Ruth could not stand the sight of her own Indian, whose Mohawk name Mercy said meant "Otter." Ruth could not bear to think that Otter owned her, but the other captives easily referred to their Indians as their masters.

Every time Ruth had to step into the woods and be private for a few minutes, she walked farther than she needed to and stayed longer. Now she stomped off the lake and into the hated forest. If only she dared escape. The closer they got to Canada, the more desperate Ruth felt. She could not be a slave, she could not be an Indian, she could not—

Her foot reached the edge of a crag she had not seen and did not expect.

In the moment of pitching over the cliff, Ruth abandoned hate and thought only of life. She scrabbled frantically. She was just flesh that wanted to go on breathing, and instead would be smashed bones on rocks below. "No!" she cried. "Please, Lord!"

The hand that closed around her and kept her from going over was the hand of the Indian who had slain her father. For a moment they stood balanced on the icy rim, until Ruth let her anger come back. "You murderer," she said, spitting on Otter. "I should have let myself fall before I let you catch me!" She jerked free and shoved him away.

He fell soundlessly over the precipice.

Thou shalt not kill.

Ruth lay down and inched forward until she could look over the edge of the cliff to see what had happened.

The force of Otter's fall had brought snow and rock down upon him. One hand stuck out, and part of his face.

But I say unto you which hear. Love your enemies, do good to them which hate you . . . And unto him that smiteth thee on the one cheek offer also the other.

What could Jesus have been thinking when he said that? This enemy was the murderer and slaughterer of innocent women and children. Ruth was not going to love him, she would never do anything good unto him, and certainly she was not going to offer him yet another chance to strike her in the face.

She rejoiced that this enemy had no choice about living or dying, any more than her father and brother had had a choice about living or dying.

She thought of her mother, giving water to the wounded French officer, and for that gesture, being left behind. She wondered how Mother felt now, alone in a world where her men had died to save her while she helped their enemies.

The savage was alive, trying with that one hand to dig himself free. A rim of ice fell like knives upon him. Ruth cried out. The Indian made no sound.

Ruth scuttled backward, out of his sight. She could go get help. Or let him die.

It wasn't fair! It wasn't supposed to be Ruth who had to love the enemy. That was just a verse you repeated in meeting. She was not going to take it seriously, loving her enemy.

But it was the Word of the Lord.

The Twenty-third Psalm moved through her mind, as warm and sure as summer wind. *He maketh me to lie down in green pastures.*

If she broke the commandment and failed to love her

enemy, she would never lie down in green pastures. Not on earth, not in her heart, and not in death.

Ruth worked her way through tangles of thin saplings and around boulders. She slid down rock faces. Sweating and sobbing over terrain that could not have been made by God, only by devils, she reached Otter at last. Her bad lungs sounded like sand rubbed on floors. She dug him out, not carefully. She might have to save him but she would not spare him pain. He was bleeding where ice had sliced him and by now her mittens were shredded, and their blood mingled, flecked scarlet on white snow.

When he was finally on his feet, she said, "It's not because I wanted to, you know."

Otter took a short careful step and paused in pain, Ruth thought, though pain did not show on his face. "It's so I won't be a killer like you," she said.

He snapped a branch in his strong hands to use as a cane. Laboriously, they made their way up the cliff, crawling part of the way.

"Actually, I hate you," said Ruth. Huge hot tears fell from her eyes and she knew that hate was not as simple as that.

Nor were the commandments.

THEY REACHED A RIVER where the water was open, seething and churning over rocks.

We're going to cross that? thought Mercy. It's too wide and deep. We'll drown.

Tannhahorens took off his tobacco necklace. He loved to smoke, as did all the warriors. Since they smoked only when they had time and felt safe, the prisoners also loved it when the men smoked; it meant everybody had time and was safe.

Tannhahorens poured tobacco into his palm. He lifted it toward the sky, calling as the loon called, his voice shivering through the wilderness. Then he faced the river and held, it seemed to Mercy, a conversation with the river. Finally, over the sharp rocks and ripping current, Tannhahorens threw all his tobacco. Every Indian did the same.

The captives stared.

Eliza, who had not spoken once since her husband was struck down, said, "It's an offering. They give their best to the river, and hope the river will give its best to them."

They walked upstream, fighting thickets and snarling brooks. When the Indians stopped to kick at a great melting drift, Mercy was too tired even to wonder.

Snow covered a dugout canoe. Forty or fifty feet long, it had been made of one great pine, the center core burned out and chiseled clean. They would paddle the rest of the way.

Mercy lay on fur on the bottom of the dugout, the sounds of water above her head, for she was lower than the surface of the river. Not having to carry her own body was joy. The loons called back for hours, wailing a long wandering cry, like a bell that would not stop ringing or a sob that would not stop weeping.

Tannhahorens said to Mercy, "It is the speech of the north," and Mercy understood.

That wild terrifying beautiful cry was the sound of where she was going.

Chapter Six

The dugout pulled up to a stone jetty and an Indian town, out of which Indian women and children poured. For a month, Mercy had prayed to reach the end of the journey, and all she wanted now was to be back in the wilderness, with only cold and hunger to worry about.

People flooded over the captives; an entire town running like water over the fields and onto the jetty, raising their arms in proud salute. Mercy tried not to show her terror.

Why *had* the Indians taken captives?

What would happen next?

Lord, Lord, she said, asking Him to be with her and keep her brave.

Since her mother had died, Mercy had been an adult in her household; bringing up her brothers; making meals; caring for babies. She had not thought of herself as a child, nor had she been one. Now she knew herself to be eleven years old, small and thin and easily defeated. She could not imagine what these alien people planned to do with her.

She looked to Tannhahorens for help, but he did not glance at her. The man who had lifted her over creeks and fed her parched corn did not exist in front of his people. Mercy had forgotten that what Tannhahorens really was, was a triumphant warrior returning home.

Tannhahorens held up scalps.

Thorakwaneken held up scalps.

Otter and Great Sky and Cold Sun held up scalps.

Eben could not stifle a groan, and Sarah Hoyt, who was closer to Eben than Mercy, put her hand lightly over his. One of the scalps was the heavily braided chestnut-red hair of Eben's older sister.

The crowd of women and boys and old men whooped continually. It was not the same sound as the howls during the assault; if screams were speech, this was different speech. But it was equally frightening.

"They're busy," whispered Ruth. "Let's just paddle away."

Joseph and Eben managed to laugh. The dugout was tied to the wharf and there were dozens of warriors within a few yards. Eben did not want to be dragged out of the boat, so he was first to step onto the jetty. He coaxed the girls to follow him. "Don't look at their faces," he said quietly. "Look beyond them at the village."

The land sloped gently up from the St. Lawrence River, and the village—much larger than Deerfield—was filled with long narrow houses with rounded roofs and no windows. The town was enclosed on three sides by its stockade, while the river formed the fourth side of protection. Beyond the town, muddy and patchy with old snow, were fields for corn. To the east of the town were stone buildings, quite beautiful and quite high. In Deerfield, stone was for foundations and wood was for buildings.

Alongside one of the stone houses stood French soldiers and above their heads flew a French flag. Its graceful gold fleurs-de-lis snapped lightly in the wind.

Mercy's heart hurt.

She was truly and fully defeated. This was enemy territory. In this place she had two enemies: the French and the Indians. The English flag with its fierce lions, she might never see again.

The crowd descended on her, fingers exploring her yellow hair, black eyes staring into the blue of her own. Mercy got separated from the other captives. She prayed for them: for Eliza to stay stupefied, so she did not know what was happening. For Ruth to stay quiet, so she did not make things worse. For Sarah to stay brave—but Sarah would do that without Mercy's prayers.

Lord God, she prayed—and outside the stockade, between the village and the garrison, Mercy saw a church.

She had known that these were Praying Indians, but she had not realized there would be a church. Puritans did not have churches. No building made by man could be sacred. They had meetinghouses and used them to discuss broken fences or ammunition shortages as well as to worship.

Made of stone, gray and strong and serious, the church was where it should be, on a hill and closer to heaven. The roof was sharply pointed, as a roof was meant to be, instead of rounded like those of the Indian houses. On its peak was a cross. Mercy fixed her eyes on the cross. She would never wear one, like Tannhahorens, which would be a sin, but if she happened to see the cross in the sky, that would be God's will.

Lord, stay with me, prayed Mercy Carter.

THERE WERE SPEECHES, none of which Mercy could follow.

There were presentations of prizes taken from Deerfield, distributed with much hollering and stomping. There went the flintlock musket Sarah had held, with her father's initials carved in the wood. There went the packet of Benny's fishhooks and the pewter cider mug that belonged to the Catlins. There was the shiny dark red quilt stitched in England by Eben's grandmother: countless tiny stitches forming a garden of puffy flowers and climbing vines.

The Indian women exclaimed over it. They knew what it was to put that many stitches into cloth.

One of the prizes was Joseph. In his Indian clothes, you could hardly tell he was English, and they walked him through the crowd to be petted and stroked.

People drifted up and wandered off and Mercy caught a glimpse of Joseph's sister Rebecca standing on the edge of the crowd with two Indian women! And then, far to the rear, Eunice Williams! So she had not fallen off her sled. The other parties must have moved more quickly—found more game, perhaps—or taken a better route. And there was Sally Burt, still huge, and her husband! Who would have thought Sally could survive?

Mercy caught their eyes, one by one. *Be brave*, they seemed to say. *It's not so bad.*

But for Eben, who in height and weight and strength was a man, it was going to be so bad.

Tannhahorens and Thorakwaneken walked off the jetty to smoke and laugh with warriors they had not seen in weeks. Then the captives were prodded out onto the packed dirty snow and arranged in a line.

From here, Mercy could see that this town was far more of a fort than Deerfield. Not only was the soldiers' garrison up high, and made of stone so it could never burn, but hanging over the water were three cannon, black holes staring grimly. Were the English ever to be so foolish as to sail north from Boston, hoping to defeat the French here, their ships would be blown to pieces.

The Indians drew back, forming lines of their own, and the captives knew this was the moment. Eben was taking deep breaths, trying to prepare himself. Sarah was fighting tears. They knew better than to cry, even Ruth. They must show as little emotion as possible.

"It's all right," said Eben quietly to the girls. "It evens the score."

"Only God can do that!" whispered Ruth, as if she had forgotten Molly and Mary and Hittie; as if she did not know the agony in Eben's heart. "It was torture enough to have witnessed the slaughter of our families. Not to mention marching three hundred miles in winter. How dare they do anything else?"

Sarah disagreed. "That wasn't torture. For the Indians, it was routine."

But Indians were not drawing back to demonstrate their cruelty on Eben's flesh. They were showing respect for a man slowly approaching over the trampled snow. Mercy knew it had to be a man, because of the silver-threaded black beard, and because of the beard she also knew he was not Indian. They did not have beards. But the man wore a gown like a woman and its black hem trailed and flowed where the snow rose and dipped.

"A Catholic priest," whispered Ruth. "He prays to a Pope instead of to God. He is going to hell. Do not speak if he talks to you. Do not meet his eyes."

Naturally they wanted to study a man who was going to hell, and even Ruth ended up staring. His beard had not been left to grow by itself, the way Deerfield men wore theirs, some patchy, some full or curly. His was clipped short and gave him dignity.

The priest's belt seemed to be made of silver and gold, tasseled like corn. On his chest hung a cross studded with brighter beads than anything Mercy had ever seen, like ice cut in chips, glittering with color.

"Precious jewels," exclaimed Ruth. "So *that's* what they look like. Isaiah 61:10," she quoted. *"As a bride adorneth herself with her jewels."*

Mercy's mother had always quoted chapter and verse. She had known the Bible as well as Mr. Williams. But Mother had been a Puritan bride, and no Puritan bride ever adorned herself with jewels.

The priest greeted the returning warriors, and to the astonishment of the captives, Tannhahorens and Thorakwaneken, Otter and Great Sky and Cold Sun knelt before him. The priest prayed in a language the English children did not recognize. It was not Mohawk, it was not English, it had none of the sounds of French. What could it be?

The priest extended his cross to the end of its heavy

gold chain, and each warrior, as he rose to his feet, *kissed* the cross. Mercy was aghast.

The crowd bowed their heads while the priest moved his arm in magical circles to finish his show. He *is* going to hell, thought Mercy.

And then, not only did the Catholic priest speak to the captives, he spoke in English. "My children, do not be afraid. I am Father Meriel. I will be your priest. Were you hard used on your march up north? Did you suffer much?"

A Frenchman cared if they were all right? A Frenchman who was a sinner, who had a Pope?

"They will not treat you so harshly now," said the priest. "Already, your people will be trying to arrange a ransom. You will stay here for the time being. I will try to arrange your purchase by good French families. Your Indians have already sold one of you to me." He put his hand on Eliza's hair, an odd, open-palmed gesture, which also seemed full of magic; as one calling on his Pope to enter Eliza. Mercy shivered.

"You will live with the nuns in Montréal," Father Meriel said to Eliza. His voice was gentle, so perhaps he had been told her history. "I will take you now. For the rest, I will see you every week when I come to say Mass and you will tell me if you need me."

Mercy locked her fingers together lest she throw her arms around his hidden knees and beg to be taken also.

She touched his robe, even though Ruth would yell at her for that, and said, "What are nuns, sir? Will Eliza be safe? She isn't very well. Will they take care of her? She doesn't talk very often. Will they be kind?"

Behind his beard she could see the hint of a smile. "And what is your name?"

"Mercy Carter."

"Marie Cartier," he said in French.

"Mah-ree Cah-tee-ay," Mercy repeated, as she had repeated syllables to learn Mohawk.

"I will tell the nuns what you have said," he went on in English, "and yes, they will be kind." The priest lifted his hand and moved it over Mercy's head in the magical pattern he had used for the crowd.

Ruth and Sarah backed away, horrified.

"Is that the work of the devil?" whispered Mercy. How would she get rid of it?

"It is the sign of the cross. I am blessing you. See?" He did it again. "I am drawing a picture of the Father, Son and Holy Ghost. His peace will go with you."

He turned to bless the others, arm and palm still up, and Ruth said fiercely, "Do not do that again. I will leap into the river and wash it off if you try to paint your cross over me."

He looked at Ruth tenderly. "The current is strong. Do you hear roaring? Rapids are downstream. You would be dashed against the rocks. Pray to the Lord for patience and He will bring you home."

What did Ruth possess, Mercy wanted to know, that no matter how rudely she spoke, everybody liked her for it?

Father Meriel headed back toward his stone buildings, pausing to paint the cross above every Indian who spoke to him. He walked more slowly than an Englishman would have. Deerfield men, including the minister, had crops to plant and animals to tend, weather to fend off and firewood to lay in. Deerfield men were in a hurry. Father Meriel floated, like a hawk on the wind.

A hawk, of course, with sharp eyes and sharper beak, would soon drop, going for the kill.

MERCY FOUND HERSELF escorted by a grown woman on either side of her. Where was Tannhahorens? Had he given her away? Sold her? Lost interest? Did she have to do this alone? If only she could hold Daniel while she walked here! Where was Daniel? Was he safe?

Row after row of windowless bark huts spread out before her. Doors were hanging flaps of skin and instead of chimneys there were holes in the roof. Smoke rose in lazy curls.

Her heart burst with worrying about Sam and John and Benny. Had her brothers gone alone into some Indian town like this? Did they have each other? Had they been sold or abandoned? Or, like Joseph, were they being made much of and given honorable names such as Sowangen?

Could Father Meriel really call the peace of the Lord into her heart? She certainly needed it.

Finally the women stopped, lifting a deerskin door, and they and she ducked to enter one of the longhouses. Inside it was smoky from two bright fires, full of shadows thrown by the flames. But its frame of saplings was hung with the same things as home: smoked meat, dried corn, leggings, adze, pistol, buckets and many plates.

She wondered briefly how you could hang plates but was too tired to consider it very long.

It was blessedly warm inside and smelled of herbs and woodsmoke. From a tripod over the fire hung an iron kettle filled with stew. She could see beans and meat and corn in the gravy and was so overwhelmed by hunger she was ready to use her bare hand for a spoon.

One of the woman filled a ladle with stew for Mercy, who took it in trembling hands and swallowed desperately. It was delicious. She was so glad to taste real food instead of gnawing bones over a wilderness fire. So glad to have something with ingredients, a mixture, a variety. She was glad to be among women.

She ate standing up, hoping for a second helping, but the women shook their heads. They guided her to a sort of shelf piled with furs and blankets. When she was seated, they handed her a corn cake. It was a plain flat patty with maple syrup dribbled over it, and Mercy had never eaten anything so wonderful. She had had no bread for so long.

Then they peeled away her filthy clothing. She was too tired to be modest and when they washed her with hot water and pulled a long Indian tunic over her, the soft deerskin was so clean; so welcome. They coaxed her to lie down on the shelf and tucked her in as so long ago she had tucked Sam and John and Benny and Tommy in. Mercy had not slept in a bed for over a month.

And a roof above her.

When you lived with nothing between you and the weather, you were indeed savage, and so it took savagery to stay alive. But a roof! And walls. You could breathe again. Sleep without terror.

A hideous smell filled the room and she jerked upright, but it was medicine, a salve they rubbed into the raw skin and cracking scabs of her feet. Just as she closed her eyes to tumble into real sleep, she saw the many plates swaying slightly in the updraft from the fire.

They were scalps.

WHEN SHE WOKE UP, Mercy could not guess from the dim smoky light what time of day it might be. The woman who had given her stew was stirring food in the same pot, a little girl was playing house on the floor, making tiny lodges out of twigs and bark shreds, and two men were playing a game with stones over a pattern drawn on the dirt floor.

I will pray, she told herself. I will eat breakfast. Then I will walk out of here and go find the others. I'll talk to

Sarah and Joseph. I'll see how Eunice did on her trip. I'll find Rebecca Kellogg and Sally Burt and see if they know where John and Benny and Sam are.

It took courage to move the blanket away, swing her legs around and meet their eyes. She had thought Tannhahorens would be here, not four staring strangers and a gap-toothed little girl. How fair was it that this little girl lived, while Marah and Tommy and Molly and Mary and Hittie did not?

Mercy pulled her moccasins on. The salve had worked. Her feet felt much better.

Everything would be all right. The priest had said so. He had said that even now, her people were working on ransom. So this was temporary; she need only cooperate for a while; she would go home.

The word *home* split into pieces. She could not fathom what home might consist of right now.

Lord, Lord, she said, and He quieted her heart and told her to put her trust in Him.

Leaving the spoon in the kettle, the woman took Mercy's hand and led her outside into softly falling snow. They walked between several houses and past a wide open space that must be a common garden come spring, and then the woman stood over a trench, lifted her skirt and made water. Mercy closed her eyes with the horror of doing this so publicly, but there were no other choices, so she did the same, washing herself with snow, and they went back into the house.

After several corn cakes, Mercy felt ready to face the day until she saw that one of the men was wearing her father's best shirt: the white blouse with ruffles he saved for Sunday. The ruffles Mother had sewn with such affection, evening after evening, as Father took his turn telling stories and the boys fell asleep by the fire.

Mercy tried to find a place to look where nothing would upset her. There was no such place.

Tannhahorens appeared in the door, but Mercy hated him now and hardly looked his way. He didn't notice. He talked with the woman who had ladled out the stew, and when Tannhahorens left, the woman took Mercy's hand and led her from the house once more.

Tannhahorens had already vanished.

Ruth was right about everything, thought Mercy. We're going to be slaves, helping with Indian babies and staring up at Indian ceilings.

"Nistenha," said the woman, tapping herself to show this was her name.

"Nistenha," Mercy repeated dully.

"Munnonock," said Nistenha, tapping Mercy.

"Munnonock," agreed Mercy.

Nistenha stopped only three houses away, lifted the flap and ducked inside.

Sally Burt lay on rugs by the fire, in labor. "Oh, Mercy!" she cried. "Oh, thank God! Hold my hand. I begged them to send for you."

For me? thought Mercy, truly honored. Not for

Sarah, not for Ruth, who are older and wiser, but for me?

So Mercy sat, holding Sally's two hands, while Nistenha and the other women helped and talked in their language and gave Sally medicine to drink.

"I told myself I wouldn't scream," Sally told Mercy. "No matter how much it hurts, I am not going to scream. Indian women probably grunt once and they're done."

Sally and Mercy giggled, although Mercy was terrified. In spite of all the births happening all the time in Deerfield, she had never seen one. Women dealt with it, while children and fathers stayed far away.

But this was Sally's first, and she didn't know what it would be like either.

"Oh, no!" said Sally. "Oh, no, Mercy, it hurts so much! I'm going to scream after all!"

They giggled again, and Sally screamed.

"Did anybody hear me?" gasped Sally.

"They could hear you in Boston," said Mercy, and the girls giggled again.

But Nistenha spoke anxiously and earnestly in Mohawk. Mercy strained to understand, because it sounded important, and everything in childbirth was important. She simply could not get the words.

From outside the hut came a woman's voice, an English voice, speaking English. Who could it be? Not a

Deerfield captive; they couldn't have learned enough Mohawk that fast.

"She's telling the mother not to scream," said the voice. "If she screams, her child will be born a coward."

Nistenha put a cylinder of wood in Sally's mouth and Sally bit down so hard Mercy thought she would break off a tooth, but it absorbed the pain, and Sally did not scream again.

By now the longhouse was packed with women jabbering and offering advice, none of which Nistenha appeared to want. The room was exceedingly hot. Nistenha wiped the sweat off Sally's forehead and four rough hours later, without a second scream, Sally Burt was delivered of a boy.

Nistenha lifted the baby, cleaned him and wrapped him while Mercy stared, awed at the fragility of newborns. They wrapped Sally too in a fresh sheet of European cloth and spooned soup into her. When they finally handed her the baby, Sally unwrapped him to check. "Oh, he's beautiful!" she cried. "He's perfect! Look at him! Mercy, isn't he wonderful?"

"Nistenha!" cried the women in a chorus.

Mercy was surprised. She must have misunderstood the ladle woman's name.

Now every woman in town trooped in to admire the new baby, who was squalling and turning himself redder than any Indian. Among them was a white grandmother, who had been taken captive, she told them, thirty years ago. It was her voice that had translated for Nistenha.

Thirty years! thought Mercy. She imagined herself growing old here. No. It could not happen to her.

At last they let Sally's husband in. He was pale and shaking and loaded with presents that Indian men had given him in honor of the event. Nistenha arranged the gifts where they could be admired. Mercy was dumbfounded to see a beautiful imported wool dress, fine furs, bracelets of silver and a cradle board so delicately carved she did not think a Deerfield craftsman could duplicate it. It was not new; it had been cherished by some Indian parent for some Indian child.

How strange the Indians were. They rejoiced over this birth—they who had not let other babies live.

"Benjamin," said Sally to her husband, lifting her face for his kiss. Her joy filled the room. "Come look at our son! He's perfect! It wasn't hard at all! Everything's fine!"

Mercy could not imagine how Benjamin felt, his son born among Indians. No house for the boy to grow up in, no farm for him to work, no grandparents. Just captivity. But from their faces, neither Sally nor Benjamin cared.

She remembered the last day of her mother's life, the new baby Marah handed over to a neighbor to nurse, and Mother telling Mercy good-bye. Childbirth was so dangerous. *Please, God, let Sally be fine! Please, God, let the baby stay well!*

And then in came Father Meriel, also carrying packages, which turned out to be a folding table, a white cloth embroidered in white to spread upon it, a cup of silver and a beautifully bound leather book. Mercy feasted her eyes on the beautiful things. How Mother would have loved that white cloth with its white needlework!

But there was a grim reason why ministers came to a birth. The baby must be baptized, in case he died. If he had not been baptized, God would not take his little soul. But Catholic souls were damned. A baptism from Father Meriel would be worse than letting the baby die unbaptized! And yet what if the baby died and his soul floated hopelessly for eternity? Should they let this man that Ruth said was going to hell put his magic cross on the baby? But he *was* a man of God.

Oh, how Mercy wished for Mr. Williams.

"I'm not Catholic," said Sarah, trying to hide the baby under her sheets.

Father Meriel opened his leather book. It was a church record for a name and a date in order to preserve the child's soul forever and ever.

Sally's husband Benjamin touched the book, overwhelmed by fear for his little boy. "Yes. Baptize him, please, Father Meriel," said Benjamin. He looked desperately at his wife, who after several amazed and horrified moments nodded.

"His name will be Christopher, then," said Sally.

"Bearer of Christ. Will you say it in English as well as French, Father Meriel? I want it to hold."

"I will say it in four languages," said Father Meriel, "for you are among Indians who also love your son. And I promise that it will hold."

"But," said Mercy, although it was rude to interrupt, "that's just three languages. English, French and Mohawk."

"Marie," he said, remembering her with a smile. "The church has yet another language. It is called Latin."

And there, in the hut of Mohawk Indians, an English Puritan was baptized in Latin by a French Catholic priest. And then baptized in French, in Mohawk and finally in English.

The baby was safe.

The baptism would hold. The whole room felt it and knew it.

"Thank you," whispered Sally.

When the priest had packed up and most of the women had left and the men had taken Benjamin out with them, Mercy asked, "Father Meriel, what does *nistenha* mean?"

"It means 'mother.' "

"How nice!" said Sally, breaking into another glowing smile. "They were all congratulating me on being a mother! Christopher," she crooned to her son, "I'm your *nistenha*."

The woman who had called herself Nistenha was

folding the messy delivery cloths and putting them in a basket to carry away, probably to wash in the river.

How dare you! thought Mercy. Do you think you can adopt me? Do you think I will cave in as easily as Sally and Benjamin caved in to that Catholic priest? Do you think I will throw away my real mother? Do you think I will ever call you by that sacred name?

She stumbled outside to cool her angry heart. She took care to avert her eyes from the French flag and the Catholic church. She turned until she was facing southeast.

I will lift up mine eyes unto the hills, from whence cometh thy help.

O Lord, send help from Boston.

Ransom us.

Chapter Seven

The town was Kahnawake and the river was the St. Lawrence: no soft Massachusetts brook but a thundering expanse, with constant traffic of pirogues, bateaux, dugouts and canoes bound for Montréal, a few miles downstream. There were French *voyageurs* and Dutch traders, Ottawa and Menominee Indians, Sauk and Winnebago, Potawatomi and Fox bringing their furs from the far west.

After so terrible a winter came an early spring. In canoes that held ten men, the Indians began coming as soon as the ice broke, bringing thousands of beaver pelts. Home they went, loaded with firearms and ammunition, brass and copper, jewelry and dresses for their wives, their paddles slicing vigorously through the water.

But that was the river and the city of Montréal.

In Kahnawake, the week following the captives' arrival was marked by nothing at all.

In Deerfield, men would have been out of bed before dawn, coming home for dinner at noon and for supper after dark, lamenting what had not been accomplished. The women would have woven and quilted, mended and cooked and scrubbed. Every child had chores: sewing, stirring, tending animals, minding babies. Then came Bible reading and prayers and at last, the exhausted collapse into sleep.

But here in Kahnawake, nobody did anything. Every now and then, one of the women started another pot of stew, and every now and then, somebody wandered by and ate some. The children played, the men smoked, the women talked and the babies napped.

"They are so lazy," said Ruth. "It is sinful."

Mercy felt dizzy rather than lazy. From the hard labor of Deerfield, she had passed through the ordeal of the march and fallen into what? Standing around, staring around, and eating.

The girls were at the bake ovens used by all the women of Kahnawake, dipping thin crisp corn cakes, hot off the pan, into thick maple syrup. Mercy could have eaten a hundred. She licked her fingers.

Around the girls were barns and shacks and pens for the animals. Between them and the river were more than fifty houses, arranged in loose rows, each holding two families or more. There were hundreds of dogs, hundreds of children, dozens of horses and almost twenty captives. Except for Sally and Benjamin Burt, not one of the captives at Kahnawake was an adult. Nobody knew where the parents had been taken or even if any had survived.

Behind the houses stretched fields to be planted with corn. "If you can imagine these people stirring themselves enough to plant seeds," snorted Ruth.

Closer was another field, avoided by the Indians, who yelled if anybody stepped in it while it was soft and muddy. It was nearly a mile long and a hundred yards wide, and Mercy had not figured out what made it special.

Every day Mass was celebrated, some days by Father Meriel and some days by other priests. Mass washed over her like morning fog over the river, and like fog, it burned off during the day. It had nothing in common with the services and sermons of Mr. Williams, and to Mercy, it did not feel like religion or meeting. The priest was talking to a Christian God, but since he spoke in his church language, Latin, only God could comprehend.

Mercy lived with twelve people, not so different from Deerfield—but in one room. Everything was in that room, hanging from the ceiling, stored in baskets that slid under the sleeping shelves, stacked in corners, attached to the walls or just left on the beds until it was time to lie down.

Not that anybody cared when you lay down. Or when you ate.

The family called her daughter, unless they were calling her sister, and so did the neighbors who dropped in. Indians were always dropping in. Since nobody was ever busy, it was never a problem.

"It's so disorderly," complained Ruth. "And I cannot endure the smoke. They don't even have chimneys, so the smoke just lies around and makes your eyes water."

But oddly, it was warmer without chimneys. At home, the flames went up that brick tunnel, carrying all the heat, so that you shivered only a foot from the fire. But in the longhouse, the heat lay down with you.

Of course, so did the smoke.

What Mercy could not get over was that husbands and wives lived apart.

Even after they were married the men went on living with their mothers and sisters. Wives lived with their mothers, and the children stayed with *them*. Mercy, although she belonged to Tannhahorens, did not live with him and hardly ever ate with him. She lived with Nistenha, his wife, and with Nistenha's mother, sister and brothers, and the sister's children. The men in the house, therefore, were the uncles and not the fathers. The children of these uncles lived five houses away with *their* mothers.

All her life Mercy had dreamed of marriage and having her own home, with her own hearth and loom and garden. Girls did not do that here.

And when Mercy went to sleep at night on her plank bed, the married couples did not sleep, but did what married couples did. Right there, in front of everybody, while fire still lit the room. The men went home when they were done.

Mercy did not discuss this with Ruth. She was not discussing anything with Ruth now. Throughout the march, Mercy had felt clever, possessed of sharp eyes and fine understanding. But in Kahnawake she felt dim and confused. Just when she seemed to be getting along, Ruth would throw her into a tizzy.

"You know, Mercy," said Ruth, "I never expected to live till spring, even in Deerfield."

Nobody else had expected it either.

"I am so surprised to be alive," said Ruth. "The march killed many, but it strengthened me. My lungs are better. Now I want to see fifty more springs, but oh, Mercy! I want to see them as an English girl living in an English colony, speaking English. I can hardly bear to listen to them jabbering in their savage tongue. Night and day, the word *ransom* pounds in my head."

But to the Indians, English was the savage tongue, and Mercy was not surprised when Nistenha interrupted them. "Munnonock," she said firmly, "no English."

"Yes, English!" shouted Ruth. "Do not give in to her, Mercy! As long as we refuse to be Indian, when ransom comes, the Indians will take their money and shrug. Do not let yourself matter to them! And do not dare betray your real family by letting the Indians matter to you!"

A FEW DAYS LATER, Tannhahorens brought Mercy to the stone jetty. Sarah Hoyt sat in a canoe with Indians Mercy had never seen before, while Eben stood on the dock. He had been partly stripped, his chest and face painted in stripes of black. His hair was now Indian style, most plucked out, a little bit left to pull back into a tail.

"Sarah and I have been sold," said Eben, "to masters in a town called Lorette. Tannhahorens said we could tell you good-bye."

"No!" Mercy was sick with fear. They couldn't leave her here with just Ruth! Nistenha hardly ever let her near Joanna or Eunice or Rebecca or Sally Burt. What would she do for strength and friendship? "You won't be here, Eben? Neither will Sarah?"

How could the Indians move them around so often? When would this end?

It would end with ransom, she thought. Until that day, they were booty like the white ruffled shirt. But how would Sarah and Eben be ransomed now? They'd been sold. Like horses.

"They say Lorette isn't so far, Mercy," called Sarah, trying to smile. "Lorette Indians trade in Montréal just like the Kahnawake Indians do. Tannhahorens will take you to Montréal one day. We will look for you."

Mercy managed to nod. It was from Montréal that the ransom would come, because Montréal was French headquarters.

Around Eben's neck, loosely tied, was a beautiful collar embroidered with blue and black mountains. "Will you be a slave?" she whispered.

"I don't know." He tried to smile. "In Lorette, they are Huron. Six of the dead Indians at Deerfield, including the one I killed, were Huron."

So torture had not been omitted, just postponed. It awaited Eben at this place called Lorette.

She wanted to fling herself on top of Sarah and rip away Eben's collar. She wanted to paddle down the St. Lawrence and out into the Atlantic Ocean and down the coast of Maine, to the safety of Boston. "Don't go," she mumbled.

Sarah held her English kerchief over her mouth to hide her emotions, but Eben had steadied himself and stood patiently, waiting to leave. It's worse for them, thought Mercy. They go to yet another unknown.

Mercy knew then that she would do whatever Nistenha asked of her. She did not want to be sold to strangers and dropped into the bottom of a canoe to vanish into a different tribe with different plans.

She tried to hug Eben, but he raised his hand quickly to keep her at a distance. He didn't want his new Indians to see some weeping girl clinging to him. "The Lord bless you and keep you, Mercy," he said, "while we are absent, one from another."

It was Mr. Williams's benediction, the one she had heard every Sunday of her life.

Sarah took her handkerchief from her face, turned away from Mercy and fixed her eyes on the horizon. She was not about to enter her new unknown as a weakling. So Mercy said nothing more, lest one of them break down. The unknown Indians paddled away.

She had waved when Daniel disappeared into the mountains, but she could not seem to wave after Eben and Sarah. She stood for a long time, staring at the dwindling dots that were their canoes, until Tannhahorens took her back to the house.

The act of going inside was the worst part of the day, partly because it *was* a house, and the only other house she had ever known had also been a home. Homesickness was like a knife. It cut constantly. Homesickness had become work; something to do.

Lord, prayed Mercy, *don't leave me as Sarah and Eben have. Stay here.*

THEN ONE DAY, the town stirred and moved and suddenly everybody was rushing to and fro, preparing and carrying and gathering. Huge fires were built and haunches of deer were roasted. The bake ovens were full, batch after batch of hot breads laid on woven trays.

Maple syrup was beaten into bear fat, to make a delicious salty-sweet butter.

The men painted and prepared for war.

Canoes packed with Indian men, women and children came from other towns. All had dressed in their finest. Beaver and mink and fox were mixed with English coats and Dutch jackets and French scarves. No man or woman was without jewelry: earrings and bracelets, necklaces and anklets.

Mercy knew herself to be a Puritan: a plain dress with white apron and bonnet was the only fashion she had ever known. She could not imagine wearing jewelry, but neither could she take her eyes off it.

French officers arrived, swords hanging at their left side, buttons polished and boots gleaming. The governor of New France came, and Father Meriel, and a dozen other priests.

These were greeted by the Kahnawake chief, Sadagaewadeh, who was dressed in white: soft white skins, thick white furs, tall white feathers, startling white paint. He looked to Mercy like the ghost of war. He looked magnificent.

"Savage," muttered Ruth.

Tannhahorens had painted his face differently than he had the night he stood on Mercy's stairs. She wondered if each pattern had a meaning, and if so, what was the meaning of the face paint he had used today. His cross was shining on his bare chest and his single lock of black hair had been braided vertically and pierced with feathers, so that it rose a full foot above his head.

Thorakwaneken's chest was covered by a necklace of shells and claws so large it could have been the front of a shirt. His scalps trailed behind him like the folds of a robe.

So this was how they left for war. Feasting and speeches and farewells from the French. Where would they attack now? Deerfield again? Hatfield? Springfield?

Mercy thought of her father. Samuel Carter's face and voice seemed as remote as the beginning of time. She prayed he had not stayed in Deerfield to rebuild. What if, at this very moment, he was working those fertile fields that edged the Deerfield River? Far from the stockade; far from safety. She prayed that the destruction of Deerfield had been so complete, so dreadful, that he had gone to his brother's in Connecticut.

Attack would hit some English town. And this time, when the Indians came, would the English be ready? Or would they have convinced themselves that the Indians would never come again?

The feast was preceded by prayers from Father Meriel, and Mercy had plenty to offer. *Dear Lord, in your loving kindness, don't let the Indians attack Deerfield. But since they're going to, Lord, let the settlers be ready.*

The captives gathered together, and this time nobody stopped them. Ruth was there. Eunice Williams. Rebecca and Joanna and Joseph Kellogg, all in Indian clothing, like Mercy herself. Sally and Benjamin Burt and their baby. Mercy was astonished suddenly to see Mary Harris and Mary Field, neither of whom she had even realized was in Kahnawake.

How separated we are, she thought. How carefully our Indian families keep us among Indians, rather than among other English.

Mercy could not cuddle baby Christopher, because he was in his cradle board, fastened to Sally's back by a burden strap. Mercy kissed his sweet forehead but could not hold his tiny hands (those tiny hands were what Mercy loved best about babies) because his arms had been tucked tightly to his sides. "Are they nice to you, Sally?" Mercy asked. "Your Indian family?"

Sally hesitated for a long time, and then she bowed her head. "They are wonderful to me. My own mother could not help me more with my first baby."

Even Ruth was silenced by that.

It was time for the real prayers, Mohawk prayers, from the chief. The white grandmother who had been a slave for thirty unthinkable years translated for the Deerfield children.

> *Listen, listen, listen as the words of the people*
> *ascend in the smoke of our offering.*
> *We return thanks to our mother earth,*
> *to the rivers and streams,*
> *to all herbs and plants,*

> *to winds both great and small,*
> *to the moon and stars*
> *and to the goodness of light.*
> *We return thanks to our Creator.*

It sounds just like a psalm, thought Mercy. I too return thanks to my Creator. But the Indians and I—we thank Him for different things, and we surely ask for different things.

Joseph got restless, jumping from foot to foot, until Great Sky, among the warriors, frowned at him. After that, Joseph stood utterly still, like a carving. Mercy couldn't even see him breathe.

At last the spiritual part was over and the French presence was recognized.

Sadagaewadeh, explained their translator, was greatly pleased by the attendance of so many French officers. He said, "We thank you for the pleasure you have given us this winter sending a party to avenge us against the English."

"What does he mean by that?" demanded Ruth. "We didn't do anything to him."

"You breathe," said the white grandmother.

Mercy felt sick in her stomach when she was near the white grandmother. She did not want to know the old woman's name, not in English and not in Mohawk. The thirty years, the slavery, the combination of helpfulness and bitterness, made Mercy so uneasy.

145

"This land belonged to our fathers," cried Sadagae-wadeh. "No longer do we let the cattle of our enemy eat grass on the graves of our ancestors."

It's true, thought Mercy. My father's cattle did graze on the old Indian burying ground.

"We drink war from our birth and now our young men have tasted the joy of the fight. We give thanks, O men of France, that you guided us in battle. On this day we celebrate our return to our families and the beautiful sight of our homes."

Mercy looked at the rows of windowless bark huts. In any language, then, and for any people, home was beautiful.

"Thanks be to God," whispered Sally Burt. "This isn't a *war* party. It's just a party. They're celebrating what they already did, not what they're going to do."

"Good," said Joseph. "I hope we eat soon. I'm starving."

But first the exchange of presents must occur, and in the fashion of Indians, every gift required a speech.

The French gave the Indians muskets and pistols, and a speech, and more muskets, and a speech, and chest after chest of bullets and powder. They gave bright blankets and armloads of jewelry, tool after iron tool, pot after brass pot.

"We'll never eat," Mercy said glumly. "Next we have to stand here while the Indians give the French *their* presents."

Ruth looked at her oddly. "The Indians have already given the French a present, Mercy. Deerfield."

THERE WAS VENISON AND FISH, bear meat and beaver tail. Cider and a strange delicious tea. The French had brought hundreds of loaves of real white bread and real berry jam to spread on it. They ate for hours.

At last, Mercy found out what the honored field was for, the one that had finally dried out from the mud of spring. It was a ball field.

Almost every adult Indian male stripped off his finery and played more or less naked. There were two hundred on each team. Everybody had a stick with a cup sewn on, and the game involved throwing hard balls back and forth from cup to cup, trying to reach the goal and score. Father Meriel called it lacrosse, and he placed bets and cheered the plays. There were a few white men playing, but they had been adopted and were Indians now.

Four hundred men played for hours, racing full speed up and down a court that was all but a mile long. Mercy had never seen grown men play. She tried to imagine Mr. Williams or Deacon Sheldon celebrating a victory by running around naked and throwing balls.

The women and children and guests raced up and down the sidelines with their men, cheering or booing. Nistenha collected Mercy, having seen how much English was being spoken, and Mercy found herself racing up and down too, shouting for Tannhahorens.

. . .

SPRING, or possibly the party, made everybody cheerful and energetic. Nistenha and her mother and sister began sewing tunics from hides tanned last fall and making baskets for gathering corn and berries and nuts and squash later on. It took Nistenha no more than a few hours to make a gathering basket and sometimes she whipped the reeds together so quickly she produced a basket in an hour.

Whatever else Mercy might be, she was not a slave. Nobody made Mercy do anything. Either she was considered a child—children in Kahnawake had no chores, ever—or too white and too useless to complete a task.

There was nothing to do and nobody to do it with, and Nistenha stopped letting her visit the other captive girls. She saw quite a bit of Joseph, though, because his longhouse was next door.

A boy among Indians was special. He was a person who would become a man.

Joseph was always being taken somewhere. The Indians loved to wander through the woods and over the streams, into the marshes and beyond the hills.

Joseph was already part of a group of boys who were wrestling and running and learning to hunt, and Joseph's mother let him use Great Sky's lacrosse stick, which was beautifully carved. Whenever Great Sky took him rambling, Joseph would lord it over Mercy, who never got to do anything.

Boredom forced Mercy to ask if she could help Nistenha.

By evening, she had made her first basket; a plain serviceable thing for field work. Nistenha showed off Mercy's basket to everyone who stopped by. They complimented her creation as if it were worthy of being sold in Montréal. "Daughter!" they exclaimed. "This is a fine basket."

With the excuse that she needed to show off her basket, Mercy managed to slip away and talk to Joseph, and wonderfully, his sister Joanna was with him. The girls hugged and hugged. How Mercy savored speaking English.

"Does Ruth have a new Indian name?" asked Joseph, who never glanced at the basket. "They don't call her Fire Eats Her anymore. Is she being adopted?"

"Who would adopt Ruth?" Joanna wanted to know. "You did a fine job on the basket, Mercy. I'm learning too, but my first one was pitiful."

"Thank you," said Mercy. "And Ruth does have a new name. Spukumenen, 'Let the Sky In.' "

This was the word for the opening in the roof through which the smoke rose. When the fire was low and the weather clear, you could see sky through the hole. The hole could be covered with curls of bark to keep out rain, but the Indians preferred to let the sky in.

"I'm still calling her Fire," said Joanna. "She doesn't let any sky into my life." Joanna bounded off to join

Eunice Williams. Joanna was eleven and Eunice seven, but they lived in the same longhouse and whatever happened, they had an English friend to share it with. How Mercy envied them.

Mercy's only hope for friendship was Nistenha's cousin's daughter, Snow Walker, who was a frequent visitor and pleasant enough. But Indians were less likely to talk for the sake of talk and Snow Walker hardly talked at all. Snow Walker for a friend would be like a fence post for a friend. The only friend Mercy really had right now was Father Meriel. After Mass, he never failed to greet her. "*Bonjour*, Marie."

She loved the soft musical sounds of French. How different they were from English sounds and Mohawk sounds. But it was Latin that Father Meriel was teaching her, and the first two words she learned were *Pater Noster*. Our Father.

His Bible, from which she studied, was not just printed words on a page, but had letters in gold with swirls of indigo and scarlet at the start of each chapter. "It's the same Bible your English father read to you," Father Meriel explained, "but in Latin."

Wherever Catholics were in the entire world, they did not use their own language. They used God's language, and every Catholic anywhere said *"Pater Noster,"* even the Kahnawake Indians.

Most Kahnawake could speak at least something in

six languages: Mohawk, Abenaki, Huron, French, Latin and English.

Mohawk was shaped differently than English. Names were made up of pieces of words strung together. Her own name eluded her. *Munnonock*, its *m*'s and *n*'s humming in a friendly summery way, contained syllables she had not heard elsewhere.

Father Meriel, however, called her Marie, and in his presence, so did the Indians. Every Indian had a French Catholic name as well as an Indian name. Nistenha's name in Catholic was Marguérite; her sister was Claire and Snow Walker was Jeanne.

Whether they called her Munnonock or daughter or Marie, it always seemed to Mercy that they must have somebody else in mind. The word *nistenha* did not offend her any longer. She used it to address any older woman and nothing in it seemed to mean mother.

IT WAS TYPICAL that Ruth was the most difficult captive but nevertheless the first to be taken into Montréal. Not one English child from Deerfield had ever seen a city and they were aching to visit. When she got back, Ruth came straight to Mercy's longhouse to tell her everything. Ruth plowed to a stop and stared in horror.

"They pierced my ears, that's all," said Mercy quickly.

"Mercy! You are a Puritan! You cannot adorn yourself. Rip those out."

Mercy's aunt, grandmother, Snow Walker and three friends of Nistenha's had been discussing earring choices. It was time for a trip to Montréal, said Nistenha, so Mercy could choose earrings at the French market. Indian women had whole baskets of earrings and Mercy must have at least one pair of her own.

Sadly, Mercy put her hands up to remove the earrings. Snow Walker very gently stopped her and positioned herself between Mercy and Ruth.

Instead of giving Snow Walker a shove, Ruth said, "Montréal is wonderful, Mercy. It's a real city. Wait till you see what French women wear. Their dresses shine, and they have tiny little shoes and their hair is full of ribbons, and Mercy, they even wear scent! The buildings are stone and the nuns who have Eliza live in a building four or five times as large as our meetinghouse in Deerfield. Maybe ten times larger. The nuns dress like Father Meriel. Long black gowns with hoods and white collars and huge crosses and knotted cords at their waists."

"No English," said Nistenha.

"I'll say anything I want," Ruth told her. "Anyway, nothing about Montréal matters. Even your earrings don't matter. I have news, Mercy."

"News?" My brothers, thought Mercy. She leaped up, hope racing from heart to feet. "Sam?" she whispered. "John? Benny?"

Ruth yanked her outside.

"My brothers!" cried Mercy.

Nistenha and Snow Walker came outside with them.

"I didn't see your brothers," said Ruth. "I didn't see anybody. But we'll all see each other soon. It turns out that Boston has a very important French prisoner. A man named Batiste, who has been sinking English ships for years, but they caught him. They should have hanged him as a pirate, but instead he's in jail. The French want him back. The whole reason they came to Deerfield and got so many prisoners was so they could force Boston to exchange Batiste *for us!*"

"My brothers, Ruth. Did you learn anything? Sam? John? Benny? Did you see any of the fathers and mothers? And Daniel—I've never stopped worrying about Daniel."

"Munnonock," said Nistenha sharply, "no English. Spukumenen, go home."

"My name is Ruth," said Ruth, who never cared if they got angry with her. "What right do you have to take away my language?" she snapped at Nistenha. "You're just a nasty old squaw."

Squaw was more of an English word than a Mohawk word, and it was neither polite nor friendly. Mercy didn't like hearing it used for Nistenha. Besides, Indian daughters did not talk back to their mothers or aunts. It was as bad as swearing had been in Deerfield. Mercy looked away from Ruth.

"Munnonock, go indoors," said Nistenha. "Spukumenen, no English."

"No!" shouted Ruth. "You Mohawks took my family, my home and my town. You will not have my tongue as well."

Mercy felt as if they were both slapping her face.

Ruth's eyes were fierce. She grabbed Mercy with hands that were hot and fevered. "Mercy, stop letting things happen. Tannhahorens and Nistenha want you for their daughter. You cannot let that happen. If they adopt you, they will not sell you home. You will be here *forever*. Thirty years, even! They will marry you to an Indian boy. Tannhahorens and Nistenha don't have children, Mercy. You would be their hope for sons. Do not cooperate. Remember that Tannhahorens is nothing but a murderer. Do not allow them to put earrings in your ears or baskets in your hands. Don't pray with Father Meriel. Don't kneel during Mass. *Ransom is coming*."

Chapter Eight

By summer, Kahnawake children had stopped wearing clothing.

Mercy could not get over the sight of hundreds of naked children playing tag, or hide-and-seek, or competing in footraces. The boys—naked!—went into the woods to shoot squirrels and rabbits and patridge. They used bow and arrow, since their fathers did not like them using guns yet. Even the six- and seven-year-olds had excellent aim.

Joseph didn't go entirely bare, being a little too old, but wore a breechclout, a small square of deerskin in back and another square in front, laced on a slender cord. The boys played constantly. They were stalking, shooting, running, chasing, aiming, fishing, swimming—they never sat down.

The men, however, mainly rested. They liked to

smoke and talk, and when they were showing a son or nephew or captive how to feather an arrow or find ducks, they did it slowly and sometimes forgot about it in the middle.

A Puritan must rise before dawn and never take his ease. Puritans believed in working hard. But for an Indian man, working hard was something to do for an hour or a week. After he killed the moose or fought the battle, an Indian took his ease. Hunting men and animals was dangerous; he deserved rest afterward, and besides, he had to prepare himself to do it again. A Deerfield man didn't risk much plowing a field. A Kahnawake man risked everything going into a cave to rouse a sleeping bear.

Mercy was outdoors more than she had ever been.

She had thought that after the horrifying journey of ice and snow, she would never want the outdoors again. But spring and summer were joy.

"You're not joyful because you love the outdoors," said Ruth. "It's because you don't have to be afraid of the Indians anymore. Anything they could do, they've already done." Ruth was in a terrible mood because ransom had never arrived.

Joanna said Ruth was in exactly the same mood she had always been, and if only fire *would* eat Ruth, everybody would be happier.

Every night, Mercy obeyed her uncle Nathaniel and remembered. She was careful about it, though. Some memories must not be taken out, or they brought on homesickness. It hurt to pull up the misty image of her mother sitting at the loom, smiling as the pattern of her weaving appeared. She did like to remember her father's deep voice as he read the Bible, working his way through all sixty-six books and then starting over as soon as he finished. She would remember the children falling asleep in laps; flames casting soft shadows over beloved faces. Her memories were sweet and warm. But when she shared this, Ruth demanded, "Tell me one thing sweet and warm about the attack."

Ruth was lucky to see things clearly. Mercy was losing track of who had done what to whom. Every day it seemed less important to remember the attack. Memory was passing away like morning fog, first gray, then clear, then gone.

Father Meriel called this forgiveness.

Ruth called it forgetting, and she called it evil.

Mercy also knew that they were not living in ordinary Indian ways. Her Indians were Frenchified. They were Catholic. But before any of that, they were Indian and carried with them the ancient feuds of their tribes.

Especially during ball games, when the men bet so much and played so hard, the teams divided along tribal lines. Mercy would feel, between the Abenaki and the Mohawk and the Huron, history she did not have and did not want to have.

She was always relieved when ball games were over.

They generally ended in laughter, payment of bets, men's arms around each other's shoulders as they went off the field. But not always. There were times when tempers on the playing field were tempers on a battle-field and Mercy would pray for peace.

More often, she just wasn't home. In summer, Indian women rambled as much as the men. They wandered far afield for every berry in its season. They foraged for birds' eggs and tasty greens. They went night fishing in creeks, one holding the torch to bring the fish to the surface, another perched on the rocks to spear the fish when it rose to the light. When they came home, they weeded among the pumpkins and fat dark beans and rows of tobacco.

There was no end to the sewing, any more than there had been in Deerfield. Mercy learned to shape moc-casins and get a needle through thick bear fur to make a hat. She learned how to paint designs on hides, to em-broider with European beads or with shells and feathers. She would sit outside, crosslegged like Nistenha, enjoy-ing the patient labor of needlework and the yellow heat of the sun.

Women and older girls continued to wear skirts, but tunics were stored for the summer. All the girls and women were bare-chested.

"There's no place you can look without seeing them," said Ruth grumpily.

Mercy thought about taking off her tunic in public,

but she didn't. Eunice Williams did, but she was little. Joanna was ready to do it, but she told Mercy she would wait until Ruth was not around to scold.

All the Indian boys and some of the girls loved to swim. They stayed away from the rough currents of the St. Lawrence and spent hours every day splashing in the shallows.

"Come, Munnonock," said Snow Walker. "I'll teach you. We swim like dogs and dogs do not sink. You'll like the water. You'll feel sleek as an otter." She took Mercy's hand. "Come, sister."

"Mercy," warned Ruth, "when she calls you sister, you remember your real sister, do you hear me? Your dead sister."

It was worth going into the water just to get away from Ruth's nagging. Mercy waded in, appalled by how cold it was. Snow Walker towed her around for a minute and then let go. At first Mercy couldn't take two strokes without having to stand up and reassure herself that there was a bottom, but soon she could swim ten, and then twenty, strokes. Joseph, who had been swimming with the boys, paddled over to admire her new skill.

Snow Walker coaxed them to put their heads under the water and swim like fish. Mercy loved it. Wiping river water from her eyes and laughing, she shouted, "Come on in, Joanna!" In front of Snow Walker, she spoke Mohawk. "It feels so cool and slippery inside the water."

Joanna shook her head. "I can't see where I'm going on land. I don't want to be blind in water over my head."

"Ruth!" yelled Joseph, in English so she'd answer. "Try it. I won't pull you under by the toes. I promise."

"Savages swim," said Ruth. "English people walk or ride horses."

By now, Mercy had flung her tunic onto the grass and was as bare as everybody else. When Ruth scolded, Mercy ducked under the water and stayed there until the yelling was over.

"Just wait till you get out, Mercy," said Ruth. "The mosquitoes are going to feast on your wet bare skin."

Mercy translated for Snow Walker, who said, "No, no. We grease to keep the mosquitoes away."

Joseph, of course, had been greasing for weeks, but so far Mercy had not submitted. Ruth, unwilling to see Mercy slather bear fat over her nakedness, stalked away.

"Good," said Snow Walker, giggling. "The fire is out. We are safe now."

Mercy was startled. "I never heard you use her old name."

"I don't call her Let the Sky In," explained Snow Walker. "She would let nothing in but storms."

Snow Walker's not such a fence post after all, thought Mercy. "Snow Walker, why have they given Ruth such a fine new name?"

"I don't know. One day at a feast, the story will be told."

"They'll have to gag Ruth before they tell it," said Joseph. "She hates her new name even more than she hated her old one."

They got out of the water, racing in circles to dry off, and then Snow Walker rubbed bear grease all over Mercy.

"I can't see you from here, Munnonock," said Joanna, "but I can smell you."

"Want some?" said Mercy, planning to attack with a scoop of bear grease, but Joanna left for the safety of the cornfields and her mother. Snow Walker went back in to join a water ball team.

The two white captives were momentarily alone. They switched into English.

"Mercy," said Joseph very quietly, "I'm going to be adopted."

She almost congratulated him. It was what he wanted. He loved Great Sky and Great Sky loved him. But everyone said if you were adopted, you would not be ransomed home. "Don't tell Ruth, Joseph," said Mercy anxiously. "She'll think you have a choice." In fact, a captive was not asked whether he wished to be adopted; it was the decision of the captive's owner.

"Father Meriel wants me to be baptized Catholic at the same time."

Mercy swallowed. "You do have a choice about that, Joseph. You must refuse. You would go to hell, you know it."

"Father Meriel says Catholics do too save their souls. And I like Mass." His almost Indian face stared into hers. "So do you, Mercy."

Last Sunday a visiting priest had taught the congregation a long slow repeating chant in Latin, called the Te Deum. Four hundred Indians sang it together, and Mercy's heart nearly burst at the beauty of the men's voices.

The Deerfield frontier had been hard, and God had not made it easier. Just when the sky seemed blue, the children sweet and the crop good, God would fling hail at the corn and smallpox at the babies.

But the French God slipped like a strong shadow behind the path of the Indian spirits. He was a gentler God. In Deerfield, Mercy had been taught to fear the Lord. Father Meriel wanted her to love the Lord. Still, for Joseph to become Catholic . . .

"I will keep the name I was given on the trail," said Joseph. "Sowangen."

"Eagle," repeated Mercy. It was an honorable name.

"Because from the beginning I was brave," said Joseph.

"It is so," said Mercy, and realized that she and Joseph had gone back to Mohawk. What would Ruth say if she found out Mercy's thoughts were in Mohawk? In that language the words *eagle* and *adoption* had a beauty and a resonance that made Mercy tremble. And my real mother, thought Mercy. What would she say if she knew that my head spins with Indian words? That I like Mass? That I'm happy for Joseph?

An elm-bark canoe drew up to the stone jetty and the captives turned, as always, to see who it was.

Three white men. Not priests. Nor were they dressed like fur traders. Two stepped easily out of the rocking narrow boat. French officers, Mercy decided, but not in parade dress. Just long guns slung over their shoulders.

Dugouts were so solid you could jump up and down inside the well of the boat, but canoes tipped, and passengers not used to a canoe were terrified of being dumped into the river to drown. The third man, definitely afraid of the canoe, had to be helped out.

Joseph gasped. "Mercy!" he whispered. "It's Mr. Williams!"

The minister wore French clothing, of course; his real clothing hadn't lasted so many months. But how familiar he looked! How right. How English. In a moment Mercy would hear his voice—listen to his blessing. All her questions would be answered. Mr. Williams knew everything.

Shouting and laughing, Mercy and Joseph raced along the river, across the stones and onto the jetty.

"It's me! Mercy Carter! Oh, Mr. Williams! Do you have news?" She flung herself on top of him. Oh, his beautiful beard! The beard of a real father, not a pretend Indian father or a French church father. "My brothers," she begged. "John and Sam and Benny. Have you seen them? Have you heard anything about them? Do you know what happened to the little ones? Daniel? Have you found Daniel?"

Mercy had forgotten that she had taken off her tunic to go swimming. That Joseph did not even have on his breechclout. That Mercy wore earrings and Joseph had been tattooed on his upper arms. That they stank of bear.

Mr. Williams did not recognize Joseph, and Mercy he knew only by the color of her hair. He was stupefied by the two naked slimy children trying to hug him. In more horror than even Ruth would have mustered, he whispered, "Your parents would be weeping. What have the savages done to you? You are animals." Despair and shock mottled Mr. Williams's face.

Mercy stumbled back from him. Her bear grease stained his clothing.

"Mercy," he said, turning away from her, "go cover yourself."

Shame covered her first. Red patches flamed on her cheeks. She ran back to the swimmers, fighting sobs. She was aware of her bare feet, hard as leather from no shoes. Savage feet.

Dear Lord in Heaven, thought Mercy, Ruth is right. I have committed terrible sins. *My parents would be weeping.*

She did not look at Snow Walker but yanked on the deerskin tunic. She had tanned the hide herself, and she and Nistenha had painted the rows of turtles around the neckline and Nistenha had tied tiny tinkling French bells into the fringe. But it was still just animal skin. To be wearing hides in front of Mr. Williams was not much better than being naked.

Snow Walker burst out of the water. "The white man? Was he cruel? I will call Tannhahorens."

No! Tannhahorens would not let her speak to Mr. Williams. She would never find out about her brothers; never redeem herself in the minister's eyes. Mercy calmed down with the discipline of living among Indians. Running had shown weakness. "Thank you, Snow Walker," she said, striving to be gracious, "but he merely wanted me to be clothed like an English girl. There is no need to call Tannhahorens." She walked back.

On the jetty, Joseph stood with his eyes fixed on the river instead of on his minister. He had not fled like Mercy to cover himself. He was standing his ground. "They aren't savages, Mr. Williams. And they aren't just Indians. Those children over there are Abenaki, the boy fishing by the rocks is Pennacook, and my own family is Kahnawake Mohawk."

Tears sprang into Mr. Williams's eyes. "What do you mean—your family?" he said. "Joseph, you do not have a *family* in this terrible place. You have a master. Do not confuse savages who happen to give you food with *family*."

Joseph's face hardened. "They are my family. My father is Great Sky. My mother——"

The minister lost his temper. "Your father is Martin Kellogg," he shouted, "with whom I just dined in Montréal. You refer to some savage as your father? I am ashamed of you."

Under his tan, Joseph paled and his Indian calm left him. He was trembling. "My—my father? Alive? You saw him?"

"Your father is a field hand for a French family in Montréal. He works hard, Joseph. He has no choice. But you have choices. Have you chosen to abandon your father?"

Joseph swallowed and wet his lips. "No." He could barely get the syllable out.

Don't cry, prayed Mercy. Be an eagle. She fixed her eyes upon him, giving him all her strength, but Mr. Williams continued to destroy whatever strength the thirteen-year-old possessed.

"Your father prays for the day you and he will be ransomed, Joseph. All he thinks of is the moment he can gather his beloved family back under his own roof. Is that not also your prayer, Joseph?"

Joseph stared down the wide St. Lawrence in the direction of Montréal. He was fighting for composure and losing. Each breath shuddered visibly through his ribs.

The Indian men who never seemed to do anything but smoke and lounge around joined them silently. How runty the French looked next to the six-foot Indians;

how gaudy and ridiculous their ruffled and buckled clothing.

The Indians were not painted and they wore almost nothing. Neither were they armed. And yet they came as warriors. Two of their children were threatened. It could not be tolerated.

Tannhahorens put one hand on Joseph's shoulder and the other on Mercy's. He was not ordering them around, and yet he did not seem to be protecting them.

He was, it dawned on Mercy, comforting them.

In Tannhahorens's eyes, we are Indian children, thought Mercy. Her hair prickled and her skin turned to gooseflesh. She had spent the summer forgetting to be English—and Tannhahorens had spent the summer forgetting the same thing.

Snow Walker joined the group, now wearing a skirt. In Mr. Williams's eyes, of course, she was still naked.

But Mr. Williams saw only the gathering men. He forgot Mercy and Joseph. "My daughter," he said eagerly. "My little girl. Eunice Williams. I know you have her here. I must see her. Bring her to me."

He wants news of Eunice as intensely as I crave news of my brothers, thought Mercy. He wants to hold Eunice and talk to her and know that she is well.

She thought of her real father, whom she could forget for days at a time. Somewhere on this earth he too was desperate for news about his children.

The French officers interpreted Mr. Williams's request to the Kahnawake.

"Aongote is with her mother," said Cold Sun.

"No, no. *Eunice*," said Mr. Williams loudly. "My daughter. My little girl."

"Aongote is with her mother."

"Her name is Eunice." His voice was strained and high-pitched. He sounded like Ruth. And like Ruth, he would not ask for a translation of *Aongote*. He would not believe an Indian name could have meaning. If he did know, his pain would only increase. For Aongote meant "planted." The black-haired red-cheeked English girl would grow where she was planted.

Here. In Kahnawake.

"I demand to see her!" said Mr. Williams in his pulpit voice, the syllables ringing out over the jetty and the river. "I am her father!"

Cold Sun had refused. He could not understand why Mr. Williams continued to ask. Nevertheless, he said once more, "Aongote is with her mother."

"Her mother," said Mr. Williams, "was murdered by *you!*"

Wisely, the French did not interpret this.

There was a pause. The warriors were motionless. The French were fidgety. The children were afraid and the minister lost heart.

"I am her father," pleaded Mr. Williams. "Let me see my little girl." He held out his hands to the warriors as a kneeler in Mass begs for a blessing.

Mercy's heart broke for Mr. Williams. If she could rest her eyes upon her brothers and know that they could smile and were among friends, she too could rest her heart. So Mercy said to the minister, "Eunice is fine. They treat her well. She has Joanna Kellogg to play with and two best Indian friends already. I haven't really made any Indian friends, but people are nice to me."

He stared at her as if she had been speaking Mohawk.

"My brothers," she reminded him. "Sam and John and Benny. Have you any news?"

He stared longingly into Kahnawake. No laughing red-cheeked little daughter ran toward him. He said wearily, "Your brother Sam is with the Indians in Lorette. He lives near Eben Nims. I have indeed spoken to him. I sorrow at how he falls into Indian ways. Your brother John has been taken by a French family. He becomes more French and more Catholic every day. Already he answers to the name Jean."

Mercy yearned to confide in him and tell him how hard they were all trying, how blurry the situation was. If only she could be alone with him and pour out her heart. She struggled, wondering how to explain their lives, but he burst out, "A new name is their first step in seizing your soul. Do not let them give you a name, Mercy! When the French can think of no other name for a girl, they use *Marie*. Do not yield. You are English, you are white, you are Puritan, you will be ransomed. We will go home. I am confident that the Lord is with us still."

169

Marie. Munnonock. Sister. Daughter. Mercy answered to all these names. But she did not answer Mr. Williams.

Finally she said, "And my brother Benny?"

The French soldiers were withdrawing. Mr. Williams had not noticed. "Benny is supposed to be with an Indian family near Fort Chambly. I have not been there nor seen him." He looked over Mercy's head, searching once more for Eunice.

"And little Daniel?" asked Mercy.

"Nobody knows."

Nobody knows. Oh, the horror of it: to be three years old and have nobody know where you are.

And then she thought: But somebody does know where Daniel is. Nine warriors took Daniel. One of them surely gave him an Indian mother. Somebody somewhere is caring for Daniel. And Mr. Williams hates it, but many here are caring for his daughter, too. "You've seen Sarah Hoyt, then," she said. "And Eben."

"Sarah was in Lorette briefly, but she's been purchased by a French family. She too is in Montréal. Thankfully she is not yielding to the Catholic pressure."

How scary for Sarah. A new world and a new language for the third time in half a year. Mercy was grateful that Tannhahorens and Nistenha had kept her.

The French officer punched Mr. Williams lightly on the arm and said cheerfully, "*Monsieur*, we return another day, eh?" He bowed slightly to the assembled warriors.

How careful the French were, so outnumbered.

Perhaps, thought Mercy, they wonder if they were wise to sell guns to Indians who were *their* enemies not so many years ago but who now live beside the French, enter the French church and speak the French language. No wonder the French stay in Montréal and have made it a fortress. With any misstep, Indian allies could revert to being the enemy.

Mr. Williams embraced the two children. Mercy savored the touch of his hands. Joseph remained as rigid as the wood of a dugout.

"The Lord is with you," said Mr. Williams. And then, roughly, as though he would shake them like puppies if the warriors were not so close, "But when they force you to go to Mass, do not repeat their prayers! Never touch a cross!"

"They don't force," said Joseph. "And we do repeat the prayers."

"We go every day," said Mercy anxiously. "We say the Lord's Prayer in Latin. Father Meriel says it's the same prayer."

"He lies! A Catholic priest skulks behind his religion as Indians skulk behind trees."

Mercy bent her head for Mr. Williams's blessing, having forgotten that only Father Meriel painted the cross in the air. Sometimes when Mercy left Mass she could feel the cross hovering over her.

But Mr. Williams did not bless her. He pushed Mercy

away for the second time and said harshly to Joseph, "I expect weakness in girls, but if *you* enter a Catholic church, your weakness shames us all."

Again the interpreter knew better than to interpret. Instead, he guided Mr. Williams toward the canoe. The Englishman climbed in awkwardly, supported on both sides by French officers, and then Mr. Williams, Harvard graduate and minister, put his head in his hands and wept for the daughter he had not been allowed to see. He did not look back at Mercy and Joseph. He had never asked if they were all right.

She felt gray and hopeless. "The Lord bless you and keep you, Mr. Williams," she called, but he did not hear her over the splashing of paddles, and it was Joseph who smiled gently, and suddenly Mercy knew the Lord to be all things and all languages: Mohawk. French. English. Latin. The Lord did not mind what name Mercy used, as long as she used it well. She did not think He cared whether she answered to Marie, or to Munnonock, or to Daughter. He cared if she kept the commandments.

Honor thy mother and father, thought Mercy. Have I broken that commandment? She clung tightly to Tannhahorens's hand, trying to discern the truth.

Snow Walker spit where Mr. Williams had stood.

Chapter Nine

"Today, Munnonock," said her mother, "we take you into Montréal."

Mercy danced with delight. She would be the last English child to find out what a city was.

The family was shopping for a celebration. Snow Walker's baby sister had reached three years of age. It was time to set aside her French name, Marguérite, and give her a real name: Gassinontie, which meant "Flying Legs," because from the moment the little girl had been able to walk, she ran instead.

To go into the city, Mercy wore her best deerskin leggings and a tunic heavily embroidered by Nistenha's mother. Six bracelets that belonged to Snow Walker decorated her arms. Nistenha had spent an hour braiding and greasing Mercy's hair, working beads into it. Her earrings were borrowed. Nistenha said they would look for earrings that Mercy could wear at the feast for Flying Legs.

Nistenha and Tannhahorens and all Nistenha's relations went in two canoes, and Ruth's family in another, and two more Kahnawake canoes also crossed the river to Montréal.

Instead of one small jetty, below the stone ramparts of Montréal were a dozen piers and wharves. Pirogues and flat-bottomed bateaux had tied up, and no fewer than three oceangoing vessels were there. Huge barrels and caskets were being offloaded. On the shore, safely guarded, hundreds of bales of fur were waiting to be shipped to Europe. Above this towered the immense stone convent of the nuns and the spire of the church of Notre-Dame.

The Indian men departed for their errands, and the women and children went in the gate to the markets.

The ladies strolling and shopping wore gowns that glowed in rich colors like the painted letters in Father Meriel's Bible. Their hair was curled in pillows and curves. In Deerfield, women pulled their hair up into buns and secured it with pins or hid it with bonnets. These ladies wore bright dainty slippers instead of the bootlike shoes of Deerfield. They smelled like lilacs in spring.

Like a savage, Mercy wanted to touch the French ladies' gowns.

And one of the French children was her cousin Mary. Mary's hair had been fixed somehow into rings and on her head was a tiny, silly hat. Her emerald green dress was pleated and sashed and a row of silver buttons glittered all the way down the front. She held the hand of a young Frenchwoman in a pink gown painted with roses and frothing with lace.

Mercy approached her cousin almost timidly. "Mary?" she whispered. "Mary? It's me, your cousin Mercy."

The pink lady said, "*Oh, ma pauvre petite! Mon dieu, vous êtes en sauvage.*"

My poor little one. My God, you have become a savage. In English or in French, *savage* was a word Mercy had come to dislike.

"Mercy! What's happened to you?" said her cousin. "Your skin is ruined. You look as if you haven't worn a bonnet or used a parasol all summer."

"No," said Mercy. Parasol, she thought.

Cousin Mary still had her pretty smile, her single dimple and her happy laugh. "This is my new mother, Mercy. You know what? I have a new name too. Now I'm Marie-Claire de Fleury."

Oh, poor Aunt Mary, dying on the march. Poor Uncle Nathaniel, who had known he would never see his children again. *Your parents would weep.*

"And Will?" Mercy whispered. "Have you seen your brother? Do you know where he is?"

Her cousin's voice dropped. "Hush, Mercy. We never talk about that."

Mercy was familiar with that rule.

They were joined by a Frenchman, very handsome, his jacket bright red, his scarf white, his pistol polished. He was utterly delighted by Mercy and picked her up in the air and beamed at her. "I," he told her, "am Monsieur de Fleury, father of Marie-Claire." He and his wife talked excitedly, nodding to one another and alternately embracing Cousin Mary and Mercy herself.

What a swirl of fathers and mothers. They were dead and alive, they were French and Indian and English, they were adoptive and blood, they were priests and parents.

Indeed, her Indian mother joined them.

"Beautiful child, you," said the father of Marie-Claire to Mercy. "To be savage, no. It is not good. In you, Marie Claire have a sister. With us, you will come. *Attendez*," he said sharply to Nistenha. He extended his palm to Nistenha, and on it lay a pile of coins.

They wanted to buy Mercy. They wanted to take her home. Mercy would be this man's daughter, instead of Tannhahorens's property. She would have a parasol and silver buttons. She would sleep between sheets on a real bed and eat white bread instead of venison.

Why did the French care about Deerfield children, when they themselves had trooped to Deerfield to destroy it?

Deerfield shimmered distantly, and Mercy could make sense of none of it.

Cousin Mary's father shook the coins in his hand as if

to attract Nistenha's attention. Mohawks had a great ability to place themselves elsewhere, leaving their bodies to wait out the events around them. The Frenchman might have been a tree in the woods for all the attention Nistenha paid him. She ignored the outstretched palm, gathered Snow Walker, Mercy and their bundles, and moved on without bothering to acknowledge the man.

I could be French, thought Mercy.

She looked back, but the family that had offered to buy her had already turned away, and the father and the mother walked on each side of their daughter, and there was no trace of Mary Brooks. It was Marie-Claire de Fleury whose green dress caught the sun.

And then, across a city square filled with stone, stone and stone, instead of mud, dust and dogs, Mercy saw Eben Nims and Sarah Hoyt.

Eben had gotten even taller and filled out. But of course he was eighteen now. He was sun-browned and garbed in Indian clothing. Sarah Hoyt wore an English dress, a French shawl and satin shoes. Like Cousin Mary, she was still very fair; her skin had seen no sun. Never had her auburn hair looked so lovely.

Mercy tore free of Nistenha's grasp and rushed to greet them. Eben hollered like a boy in a ball game when he saw her and Sarah whirled her in circles.

"How is Lorette?" said Mercy when they were done hugging and laughing with joy.

"Good," said Eben.

"Bad," said Sarah. "The men had to run the gauntlet. It was just as people told us. The Indians made two lines, they had clubs and sharpened sticks and whips, and Eben had to run between the lines and get hit and knocked to the ground and kicked."

"They did that to you?" whispered Mercy.

Eben shrugged. "Your brother Sam is in Lorette, you know. He is fine. He and his master built two canoes. One elm-bark and the other birch. He's proud of his canoes. Try not to worry about him, Mercy. One day you'll cross paths at a celebration."

Sam is fine, thought Mercy. How extraordinary. How can any of us be fine?

She pictured her brother: bigger, taller... and content.

"Benny we've never seen," Eben said, "but I ran into a white captive taken from Albany who lives in the same village as Benny. He says Benny is happy."

"Boys are always happy," Sarah pointed out. "They ramble and have adventures. It's different for the adult captives, though. In Lorette, two Deerfield men are slaves. They're kept on a leash and they work the fields with the women. In Lorette, only old women without teeth and slaves work in the field."

"Eben, does that include you?" said Mercy anxiously.

Eben shook his head. "No. My father is teaching me to hunt."

It was an Indian way of telling Mercy so much. He

did not consider the Indian his master, but his father. He was not a slave, but a son who must learn important things. He was not weeding and hoeing, but hunting, which was men's work.

And the gauntlet was not to be discussed. She wondered if her brother Sam had had to watch when Eben suffered. But she honored Eben's decision not to speak of it. "And you, Sarah?" she asked.

"A French family bought me," said Sarah in disgust. "They're kind, but they're not adopting me the way your cousin Mary was adopted. I despise the French, Mercy. I despise how the women live. I loathe their perfume and their frippery and their foolish parties."

"I believe you were less angry when you lived among the Indians," said Mercy.

"Indeed I was," said Sarah. "Now *ransom* is the first and the last word in my heart every waking moment, and then I dream of ransom in my sleep. I want to go home to Deerfield and be a Puritan."

I have not dreamed of ransom in weeks, thought Mercy. I have not even remembered it. She wondered how Sarah pictured Deerfield? Would Sarah actually go back to that place of death and destruction? Would she start over among the ashes? Or did Sarah believe Deerfield existed as it had before?

"They're picking out a French husband for me," said Sarah.

Of course they are, thought Mercy. You are eighteen

and beautiful and English women have sons every year. That's better than a dowry.

"Remember how in Deerfield there was nobody to marry? Remember how Eliza married an Indian? Remember how Abigail even had to go and marry a French fur trader without teeth?"

Mercy had to laugh again. It was such a treat to laugh with English friends. "Your man doesn't have teeth?"

"Pierre has all his teeth. In fact, he's handsome, rich and an army officer. But what am I to do about the marriage?" Sarah was not laughing. She was shivering. "I do not want that life or that language, Mercy, and above all, I do not want that man. If I repeat wedding vows, they will count. If I have a wedding night, it will be real. I will have French babies and they will be Catholic and I will live here all my life." Sarah rearranged her French scarf in a very French way and Mercy thought how much clothing mattered; how changed they were by what they put on their bodies.

"The Catholic church won't make you," said Mercy. "You can refuse."

"How? Pierre has brought his fellow officers to see me. His family has met me and they like me. They know I have no dowry, but they are being very generous about their son's choice. If I refuse to marry Pierre, he and the French family with whom I live will be publicly humiliated. I won't get a second offer of marriage after mistreating this one. The French family will make me a servant. I will spend my life waiting on them, curtseying to them, and saying '*Oui, madame.*'"

"But surely ransom will come," said Mercy.

"Maybe it will. But what if it does not?"

Mercy stared at her feet. Her leggings. Her moccasins. What if it does not? she thought. What if I spend my life in Kahnawake?

"What if I stay in Montréal all my life?" demanded Sarah. "A servant girl to enemies of England."

The world asks too much of us, thought Mercy. But because she was practical and because there seemed no way out, she said, "Would this Frenchman treat you well?"

Sarah shrugged as Eben had over the gauntlet, except that when Eben shrugged, he looked Indian, and when Sarah shrugged, she looked French. "He thinks I am beautiful."

"You *are* beautiful," said Eben. He drew a deep breath to say something else, but Nistenha and Snow Walker arrived beside them. How reproachfully they looked at the captives. "The language of the people," said Nistenha in Mohawk, "is sweeter to the ear when it does not mix with the language of the English."

Mercy flushed. This was why she had not been taken to Montréal before. She would flee to the English and be homesick again. And it was so. How she wanted to stay with Eben and Sarah! They were older and would take care of her . . . but no. None of the captives possessed the freedom to choose anything or take care of anyone.

It turned out that Eben Nims believed otherwise.

Eben was looking at Sarah in the way every girl prays some boy will one day look at her. "I will marry you, Sarah," said Eben. "I will be a good husband. A Puritan husband. Who will one day take us both back home."

Wind shifted the lace of Sarah's gown and the auburn of one loose curl.

"I love you, Sarah," said Eben. "I've always loved you."

Tears came to Sarah's eyes: she who had not wept over her own family. She stood as if it had not occurred to her that she could be loved; that an English boy could adore her. "Oh, Eben!" she whispered. "Oh, yes, oh, thank you, I will marry you. But will they let us, Eben? We will need permission."

"I'll ask my father," said Eben. "I'll ask Father Meriel."

They were not touching. They were yearning to touch, they were leaning forward, but they were holding back. Because it is wrong? wondered Mercy. Or because they know they will never get permission?

"My French family will put up a terrible fuss," said Sarah anxiously. "Pierre might even summon his fellow officers and do something violent."

Eben grinned. "Not if I have Huron warriors behind me."

The Indians rather enjoyed being French allies one day and difficult neighbors the next. Lorette Indians might find this a fine way to stab a French soldier in the back without drawing blood.

They would need Father Meriel. He could arrange anything if he chose; he had power among all the peoples. But he might say no, and so might Eben's Indian family.

Mercy translated what was going on for Nistenha and Snow Walker. "They want to get married," she told them. "Isn't it wonderful?" She couldn't help laughing from the joy and the terror of it. Ransom would no longer be the first word in Sarah's heart. Eben would be. Mercy said, "Eben asked her right here in the street, Snow Walker. He wants to save her from marriage to a French soldier she doesn't want. He's loved Sarah since the march."

The two Indians had no reaction. For a moment Mercy thought she must have spoken to them in English. Nistenha turned to walk away and Snow Walker turned with her.

If Nistenha was not interested in Sarah and Eben's plight, no Indian would be.

Mercy called on her memory of every speech in every ceremony, every dignified phrase and powerful word.

"Honored mother," she said softly. "Honored sister. We are in need and we beg you to hear our petition."

Nistenha stopped walking, turned back and stared at her in amazement. Sarah and Eben and Snow Walker stared at her in amazement.

Sam can build canoes, thought Mercy. I can make a speech. "This woman my sister and this man my brother wish to spend their lives together. My brother will need the generous permission of his Indian father. Already we know that my sister will be refused the permission of her French owners. We will need an ally to support us in our request. We will need your strength and your wisdom. We beseech you, Mother, that you stand by us and help us."

The city of Montréal swirled around them.

Eben, property of an Indian father in Lorette; Sarah, property of a French family in Montréal; and Mercy, property of Tannhahorens, awaited her answer.

"Your words fill me with pride, Munnonock," said Nistenha softly. She reached into her shopping bundle. Slowly she drew out a fine French china cup, undoubtedly meant for the feast of Flying Legs. She held it for a moment, and then her stern face softened and she gave it to Eben.

Indians sealed a promise with a gift.

She would help them.

From her bundle, Snow Walker took dangling silver

earrings she must have bought for Mercy and handed them to Sarah.

Because she knew that Sarah's Mohawk was not good enough and that Eben was too stirred to speak, Mercy gave the flowery thanks required after such gifts.

"God bless us," she said to Sarah and Eben, and Eben said, "He has."

Chapter Ten

Mr. Williams's second visit occurred in the morning before the celebration for Flying Legs.

Again he came with soldiers, stood on the jetty and begged to see Eunice. Again the Indians said Aongote was with her mother.

Mr. Williams argued.

Cold Sun listened politely.

Ruth stormed up and Mercy edged closer, while guests arrived in canoes and dugouts, bearing gifts and food.

Mr. Williams seemed not to notice the extraordinary differences in hair and dress and tattoos that marked one tribe from another; not to hear the astonishing flow of many languages and the shouts of greeting.

Sadagaewadeh, the chief himself, had been coaxed by the French to discuss the problem of Aongote. The

chief, however, did not believe in discussion. Sadagaewadeh said that the last time Mr. Williams came, he
had made Munnonock cry. Therefore he might make
Aongote cry. Therefore he must go back where he had
come from.

"Mercy cried because she was glad to see me!" said
Mr. Williams, but Indians did not cry for such a reason.

Aongote is safe and happy, Mercy wanted to say, but
Mr. Williams did not want to hear that. Children
should be safe and happy only with their own parents.

"Eunice is doing all too well, Mr. Williams," Ruth
said grimly. "She is sliding so fast into being a savage
you would not recognize her."

Mr. Williams failed to be grateful for Ruth's infor-
mation.

Ruth alone among the captives had fought wearing
Indian clothing. When they had reached Kahnawake last
spring, her wool skirt and blouse had been shredded and
stained, but she would not exchange them for deerskin.
As always, Ruth had triumphed. Her Indian family had
gone into Montréal and bought her French clothing. So
while Mercy wore deerskin, Ruth had flounces and ruffles, a yellow silk cape and a mauve bonnet to keep off
the sun.

"They won't let you see her," said Ruth flatly. "Now
tell us, Mr. Williams, why has ransom not come? Do
people have short memories or no memory? Why do
they not rescue us? I get so angry sometimes."

187

Sometimes! thought Mercy.

"Our sins provoke God to do dreadful things," said their minister sadly.

Does he mean that ransom will not come because we are still sinners? thought Mercy. She knew she sinned. She participated in Mass. She laughed with her Indian family. Was she, Mercy Carter, preventing ransom?

They were jostled by shrieking Indian children vaulting out of a dugout and racing into the village to see what there was to eat.

"You know what else they're celebrating today?" Ruth said to Mr. Williams. "Along with giving out a savage name to a little girl? The Indians attacked an English village in Maine. They caught the settlers unaware, just like us. Took scalps. They'll be showing them off."

Mercy's heart sank. She had not known this. At least it couldn't have been Tannhahorens, she thought. Or Thorakwaneken. Our men haven't gone anywhere.

She caught her thoughts. *Our* men. No, no, she corrected herself. *Our* men are the white settlers.

"My children," Mr. Williams told them when he was forced to leave without seeing Aongote, "do not surrender. Think constantly of home. Our task is to *get* home, not make *this* home."

He was looking at Mercy and seemed even sadder.

HUNDREDS DANCED after the feast, arranging themselves in long lines, endlessly repeating the same steps.

The foot patterns were simple: left left, right right, left right. Toe toe, heel heel, toe heel. The rhythm poured down Mercy's bones and shook through her feet. How she loved the drums and rattles and clappers.

Mercy ached to dance. But she kept herself still. Think of home, Mercy reminded herself. Puritans do not dance. Dancing is a sin. Do not surrender.

Snow Walker was dancing more on one side of the line than on the other. Her face turned far more often to her left than to her right.

Mercy studied the line. A dozen dancers to Snow Walker's left was a young warrior named Garionatsigoa, Great Angry Cloud. It was an honorable name whose history Mercy did not know. But he certainly did not look angry now. He was as captured by Snow Walker as Eben had been by Sarah.

Snow Walker danced out of line and over to Mercy. "It's all right to dance, Munnonock. Anyway, Fire Eats Her went back to her house. No one will tell on you. Come. Dance with me."

Snow Walker's face was bright with vermilion borrowed from her father's war paint and her arms were decorated with circling rows of tiny dots, like a hundred bracelets. Her black hair was woven spectacularly with bear claws. She wore a new tunic painted with leaping red stags.

She was beautiful.

Mercy danced. How wonderful it was!. Her feet

shouted to the ground and every beat of the percussion seemed meant just for Mercy.

Snow Walker whispered, "Is he looking at me?" She tilted her head toward the young brave.

"Yes," said Mercy. "He's looking at you."

They stamped and spun. Every half turn, Mercy and Snow Walker shifted one place closer to Great Angry Cloud.

Dancing was a sin, and she knew it, but the dark fear that used to descend over Mercy when she offended the Lord did not come. The Lord was not ignoring her dance; it was more that He saw no offense to worry Him.

MERCY'S SECOND TRIP to Montréal was on a raw and chilly day when the wind off the river bit her skin and hurt her eyes. Nistenha had lost all her metal fishhooks in the course of the fishing season and wanted to replace them.

It was a large party that went shopping: Snow Walker, Joanna, Mercy, Eunice Williams and all their mothers. Mercy was a little surprised that Eunice was going. Mr. Williams was known to be in Montréal; he had been purchased by the French, who let him come and go as he pleased within the city. But Ruth was correct: Eunice had slid so completely into being a savage that Mr. Williams would not, in fact, recognize her. She was just another small Indian. She really was Aongote.

The mothers loved shopping. Wrapped in their blankets and cloaks, they fingered every strange object, exclaiming over it, rejecting it, laughing at it or negotiating for it. Joanna, Eunice and Snow Walker were equally eager to go into every shop and inspect the goods of every vendor.

But Mercy scanned the crowds. Running into Eben and Sarah had been like being reborn. There were so many captives she'd never seen again; so much news she yearned for. Perhaps a little boy would dart from the crowds and she would recognize Daniel. And one beautiful day, surely, she would see her brothers Benny and Sam among the Indians, and John among the French.

And so while the others were admiring themselves in looking glasses to see what color wool they liked best, Mercy studied the passersby. Many buildings had high stone steps and Mercy climbed up to get a better view.

The person she recognized, however, was Eliza, the widow of Andrew, walking between two nuns. French syllables spilled among them. Eliza, safe and happy. Talking easily.

Mercy leaned out toward Eliza as, a lifetime ago, she had leaned out her bedroom window toward the hills of Deerfield and seen the taking of Zeb and John. And just as she had said nothing that time, she said nothing now. Why remind Eliza of Deerfield and the terrible death of Andrew?

Mercy dropped her eyes so Eliza would not see her

before she remembered that the golden hair that usually gave her away was covered by a fur cap. She too was merely another Indian. There was not a risk that the nuns or Eliza would even think of examining her.

Nistenha bought everyone a hot French pastry from one street cart and sweet hot tea from another, while Aongote's mother tried to come to a decision on wool colors.

Mercy slipped away, threading through the crowds to the center of the square, and stopped short.

Not ten feet away, Mr. Williams was arguing with a Jesuit priest. They looked almost identical, their arms flailing, deep frowns marring their faces.

Mercy was back among the Indians in a moment, whispering to Aongote's mother, "Aongote's white father is coming this way. See him with the priest?"

Aongote's mother set the woolens down without buying anything. "Come, daughters," she said calmly. "We go back to the wharf."

"Oh, let's stay longer," pleaded Aongote. "I wanted the yellow cloth. And I thought we were going to church to hear the trumpet. You told me all about the trumpet."

"Another day," said her mother, taking her hand.

They did not hurry and the high disappointed voice of Aongote continued. But Mr. Williams would not recognize the voice, because Aongote spoke in Mohawk, and he would remember only Eunice speaking in English.

At the wharf, all three oceangoing vessels were now loading fur for the return voyage to France. There was great wealth here. Beaver skins were distinctive: flat ovals of soft shining brown. Their bales were smaller than bales of other skins, but all hides stank, and the smell of the ships was intense. The Atlantic was dangerous to cross in winter. The longer they waited, the greater the risk. They must set sail soon.

Nistenha piled furs on the bottom of the dugout's deep well and told Joanna, Aongote and Mercy to take naps. Aongote was grumpy but obeyed after a sharp look, curling at her mother's feet and vanishing from sight. Joanna and Mercy tucked themselves at the other end, while the mothers and Snow Walker sat up patiently to wait for the men. The women seemed happily entertained by the ships. Nobody asked Aongote's mother why it had been necessary to leave so quickly.

Joanna breathed in Mercy's ear, "Why did you do that? It was mean and wrong. You know her father would give anything to see Eunice!"

"How did you know Mr. Williams was there?" Mercy whispered back. "You can't see that far."

"I heard you tell on him. Mercy, that was her father! Eunice loves him. She needs to see him. Just as we need to see our fathers."

Mercy buried her face in the mink blanket. She had committed a terrible sin. *She had been a dutiful daughter to the wrong set of parents.*

Mercy had let herself believe that Eunice *was* Aongote and her father *was* Cold Sun—not Mr. Williams. She had let herself believe that Nistenha and Tannhahorens were—

In one terrible cold moment, Mercy Carter understood what the name Tannhahorens meant. It meant "He Splits the Door."

She muffled her scream of rage and comprehension against the mink.

At some point in his warrior life, Tannhahorens had taken a hatchet to a wooden door and broken through. It must have been a great event, presumably with many scalps, to deserve a new name in its honor. The scalps could have been Iroquois, but Iroquois doors, like Kahnawake doors, were curtains of skin. It did not take a hatchet to break an Indian door. So every time Mercy said his name, she honored the moment that her master had smashed through an English settler's door. And into his house. And into his head.

The waters lapped, the cold wind blew, the bales were hoisted into holds and the sun lowered.

At last Tannhahorens and the others returned. Mercy feigned sleep, and the adults maneuvered around her. She could not look at Tannhahorens. She could not look at herself: not just becoming Indian—but betraying the English.

The boats crossed the water under a sky black and moonless and strewn with stars. Nistenha entertained the girls by naming the star families living in the sky. The Indian syllables tumbled and fell, and having understood *Tannhahorens* at last, now Mercy understood *Munnonock*.

Alone Star.

She flopped on her back on the mink rug and stared straight up. Many stars in that black sky also lay alone, far from their brothers and sisters; not part of a family.

Lord, no! cried Mercy in her heart. That's a terrible name, a cruel and mean name. *Lord, save me from being a girl named Alone! Forgive my sins, especially against Mr. Williams and Eunice. Send a ransom, Lord.*

They reached the jetty at Kahnawake and piled out of the boat, gathering the many purchases. The town glowed and smoked with fires of welcome. If Mercy turned Indian before ransom came, in some dark wilderness way, she would never climb out of this prison, and it would be, as Ruth had predicted, her own doing.

Mercy lagged behind, unwilling to enter the longhouse she had actually been calling home.

Tannhahorens rarely paid attention to Mercy, because capturing prisoners was men's work, but raising them was women's. But now he turned back. "Daughter?"

Daughter!

Never.

He was no father; Indian men didn't do that. He was exactly what Ruth and Mr. Williams said. A killer. A thief of babies and children. A savage. He dared call her daughter, this man who had given her the name Alone.

She walked around Tannhahorens without speaking, an act of great rudeness that she found satisfying, and went into the house where he did not live, and which he infrequently visited. Ruth was right about that too; Nistenha and Tannhahorens were not really married because married people lived together and shared a hearth.

In the smoky half dark, Mercy thought, Why wait for ransom, which shows no sign of arriving? *Why not escape?*

She flung out of her mind the cherished word *ransom*.

Escape was a richer, finer word. For ransom, the captives must wait. They might wait thirty years, like that white grandmother.

But *escape!*

She considered it seriously.

On the second day of the march, the Indians had threatened their captives with being burned alive should there be another escape. But Father Meriel said that kind of thing didn't happen anymore, it was an empty threat. In any case, months had gone by. It was long past the time when such a punishment might occur. The only person at risk was Mercy herself.

There was no way she could retrace the three hundred miles they had followed to get here. Like the ships, she must leave by the only road that existed in Canada: the St. Lawrence River.

Those ships being loaded with beaver were probably leaving tomorrow or the next day for France. She would get passage. She did not know how yet. But it had been done once. Several years ago, a Deerfield boy named John Gillett had been captured and made a slave to the Indians here. He hadn't been adopted, just used for rough work. He had fled, boarded a ship bound for France and once there, escaped the French too. He had made his way to London, coaxed a church to pay his passage across the ocean to Boston, and from Boston, John Gillett walked home to Deerfield.

When he married, though, he wisely moved his bride south to a Connecticut farm. No Gillett would be caught in another Indian attack.

Only Carters, thought Mercy grimly.

Such an escape would be harder for a girl.

She must find a protector. Perhaps a priest returning to his French cathedral. A French wife returning to visit her mother in Paris. A kind, fatherly sea captain.

It won't be hard to leave Kahnawake, she thought. They trust me. Especially after today, warning them about Mr. Williams.

Mercy decided to act immediately, before she thought about it too long and the attempt seemed too frightening.

Nistenha was stirring the stew that had been simmering since the shopping party left in the morning. "May I go back to Montréal by myself tomorrow?" Mercy asked. "I have my two baskets of sassafras to sell. I didn't see anybody else in the market with sassafras. I want to buy presents for everybody."

Buying gifts for others was always smiled upon. And the French loved sassafras, believing that it cured anything.

"Yes, Munnonock, you may," said Nistenha.

As easy as that. Mercy marveled. Tomorrow she would escape. It would be another unknown, but it would be in the direction of freedom.

Mercy Carter was going home.

IN THE MORNING, of course, there was Mass.

Mercy was able to look at Father Meriel and see that Mr. Williams was correct. In his swishing black robes, the priest skulked around trying to grab the souls of children whose bodies had already been grabbed by Indians. You almost had me, she thought.

After Mass, the Indian men took advantage of the soft earth to dig out corn barns. These were pits the size of mass graves, to be lined with sheets of birch bark, into which hundreds of baskets of dried corn kernels would be poured. Covered with pine straw, then another layer of birch bark, and mounded with dirt, the corn would stay dry and sweet all winter.

Everything here was corn. Boiled, roasted, baked, ground, dried; combined with squash or kidney beans; with meat; with syrup.

Mercy turned her back on Tannhahorens as he dug out a corn barn. I will never see you again, she thought.

In the longhouse, Nistenha's stew pot had kidney

beans, chunks of venison and of course corn. While everybody else went to out to shell more corn, Mercy ate heavily to prepare for her escape. She would need money. Sassafras was a good excuse to go into Montréal, but it would not buy her passage.

She could hardly carry off the beaver skins stacked and waiting for Tannhahorens to sell in Albany. But lying beneath Nistenha's platform was her jewelry box. Tannhahorens was a very successful hunter and trapper, and his wife had fine adornments. Nistenha's cross was almost as magnificent as Father Meriel's. Studded with real gems, it had been bought one year when Tannhahorens came upon a great many beaver furs.

Now Mercy wondered exactly how a person "came upon" beaver furs. Did a person slaughter the trapper? *He splits the door,* she thought, raging all over again.

Mercy pulled out the jewelry box and stared down at the splendid cross. Nistenha never wore it in the fields lest the chain break. In the firelight, the facets of the jewels glowed like embers.

I can't steal, she thought. Certainly not from Nistenha. She never hurt me. I cannot pile that sin on top of my other sins.

Ruth would say: *They stole your life! Your family! Your home! Of course you can take their stupid Catholic cross.*

It was possible to enter a longhouse in silence, because no wooden door creaked, no wooden floorboard groaned, no heavy shoe tromped. Mercy was unprepared to find Nistenha at her side. Shame made it impossible to look Nistenha in the eyes.

"Yes, daughter," said Nistenha. "Wear my best cross. This is your first time alone in the city. You must look beautiful. We will be proud." Nistenha put the chain over Mercy's head and also slid six silver bracelets up her arm. They were fat bracelets, so that her arm was solid with silver from wrist to elbow.

Money, thought Mercy. I have plenty of money now.

"Come, Munnonock," said Nistenha. "Spukumenen's father awaits."

Ruth was going into Montréal? Mercy froze. She could not imagine taking Ruth with her. Ruth had never cooperated with anything in her life. Ruth would find a thousand things wrong even with this plan.

Nistenha smiled. "No. Spukumenen stays here. Even she must help with the corn. Her uncles, though, have arrived in Montréal with many furs. Her father, Otter, goes to get them and will take you. You will ride home sitting on top of much beaver." Nistenha kept fixing Mercy's hair, although it was perfect; Snow Walker had fussed with it before Mass. "Much depends on you, daughter."

Mercy said nothing to that, and Nistenha did not elaborate. Together they walked out of the longhouse, out of Kahnawake village and down the steps of the stone jetty.

She had not had to steal the cross. It had been given to her.

Chapter Eleven

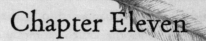

It was cold on the water.

Otter did not paddle smoothly and icy spray hit Mercy's face and arms.

She was not wearing the clothing she would have chosen. To go with the glittering cross, Nistenha had insisted upon her best tunic and her finest fur hat. Into her hair, Nistenha had woven shells and bear claws. Hardly the garb of an English girl seeking a cabin on a French ship.

Around them were another two canoes from Kahnawake, men bringing wives and sisters and mothers. Mercy managed to chat about shopping at the same time she stared down the river, holding her breath, praying the ships had not yet sailed. Finally she could make out their masts.

Her plan was still possible.

Otter tied up at one of the small jetties, and the men left to do their trading. Mercy knew by now that they were all smugglers. They claimed loyalty to the French and were always willing to help the French fight the English, but in the end, furs were sold to whatever buyer paid the most. It happened to be the Dutch in Albany. However, since the Dutch promptly sold those furs to England, it was forbidden to sell to the Dutch.

No Mohawk paid the slightest attention to the law.

The Indian women began shopping and exchanging news. There were Norridgewock and Oneida and Cowasuck Indians to talk to; there were French fur traders and jewelers and a display of glass.

Mercy traded her sassafras for a long gray wool cape with a hood. It would wholly cover her Indian clothing. The women protested vigorously; it was dull, it was ugly, Munnonock had a better cape at home. Why not purchase this pink scarf, embroidered in a riot of green leaves and white flowers?

Slowly the women separated, one going to the iron-monger, one to the shoemaker to sell him leather, one to the tattoo artist to buy needles.

Mercy turned down a lane with no shops which led past the enclosed gardens of the convent. In the shadow of the nuns' world, Mercy pulled her hair out of its braids and flung down the Indian junk tangled in it. Shells and claws. She saw herself as Ruth did; as Cousin

Mary had—a pathetic little English girl trying to curry favor with savages.

Using her fingers to comb her hair, Mercy put on the long gray cloak, and this time she did not cover her hair; its golden sheen and her blue eyes were her proof that she was English.

Then she walked back to the wharf.

SHE HAD LOST HER FEAR of small boats. After all, Indians handled canoes well and rarely went out in bad weather, and Mercy could now swim. But how alien were these great vessels, with their rope ladders and furled sails, stinking tar and shouting sailors. Their wooden bodies creaked like a hundred doors. They pulled the floating dock up and down so that everybody standing on it also bobbed and swayed.

She had heard that the sailors slept in hammocks, like Indian babies. Would they give her a cabin? Would she have a tiny room, with a tiny bed and a tiny window? Or would she too have a sling hanging from the ceiling? No matter how much beaver they had on board, no matter what profit they expected from it, surely they would want this jeweled cross as well. They could pry the gems out and set them into necklaces and earrings for their wives or sweethearts.

Mercy steered clear of the French voyageurs, who had brought the fur bales to Montréal. They were Indian lovers and might hold her until Otter came back. It was easy to recognize a *voyageur:* They thought nothing of paddling sixteen hours a day, five miles an hour. Their arms were as big as other men's thighs.

She was the only girl anywhere and the only child.

A dozen filthy swearing French sailors wrestled with barrels of water they would need for the voyage. Great tangles and whorls of rope lay everywhere. Unsold fish rotted in abandoned baskets.

She had practiced French in her mind, but now she lost the words. She could not even remember the right English words. She possessed only Mohawk.

If Otter or the other men saw her here, what would they do? If the captain did not have space for her, how could she coax him to fit her in anyway? Who was the captain? What if the captain just laughed and sent for Otter?

The dock lurched and Mercy staggered a little.

One of the sailors left the others and sauntered over to her. He was tall and thick-waisted, with a matted beard and a well-chewed pipe.

"Excuse me," she said, trying to pronounce it in the French way: "ex-cusay mwa." She tried to smile, and he grinned back. The rotting stumps of his remaining teeth stuck up like pegs next to his grayish tongue. He answered her, however, in French-accented English.

"Girl! English, eh? What is your name? Indians stole you, eh? Tell me. I'll send news to your people."

His excellent speech meant that he did a lot of trading with the English. It meant, Mercy prayed, that he liked the English. She found her tongue. "Will you take me to France, sir? Or anywhere at all? Wherever you are going—I can pay."

He raised his eyebrows. "You do not belong to an Indian?"

She flushed and knew her red cheeks gave their own answer, but rather than speaking, she held out the cross. The sun was bright and the gemstones even brighter.

The man sucked in his breath. He leaned very close to her to examine the cross. "Yes," he said. "It is worth much."

He straightened up slowly, his eyes traveling from her waist to her breast to her throat to her hair. The other sailors also straightened, and they too left their work, drawn by the glittering cross.

"So you want to sail with me, girl?" He stroked her cheek. His nails were yellow and thick like shingles, and filthy underneath. He twined her hair into a hank, circling it tighter and tighter, as if to scalp.

"You are the jewel," he said. "Come. I get a comb and fix this hair."

The other sailors slouched over. They pressed against

her and she could not retreat. He continued to hold her by the hair, as if she were a rabbit to be skinned. She could see neither river nor sky, only the fierce grins of sailors leaning down.

"*Eh bien,*" said the Frenchman, returning to his own tongue. "This little girl begs to sail with us," he told his men. "What do you say, boys?" He began laughing. "Where should she sleep? What am I bid?"

She did not have enough French to get every word, but it was the same in any language.

The sailors laughed raucously.

Indians had strong taboos about women. Men would not be with their women if they were going hunting or having important meetings, and certainly not when going off to war. She had never heard of an Indian man forcing himself on a woman.

But these were not Indians.

She let the cross fall on its chain and pushed the Frenchman away, but he caught both her wrists easily in his free hand and stretched her out by the wrists as well as by the hair.

Tannhahorens pricked the white man's hand with the tip of his scalping knife.

White men loading barrels stood still. White sailors on deck ceased to move. White passersby froze where they walked.

The bearded Frenchman drew back, holding his hands up in surrender. A little blood ran down his arm. "Of course," he said, nodding. "She's yours. I see."

The sailors edged away. Behind them now, Mercy could see two pirogues of Indians drifting by the floating dock. They looked like Sauk from the west. They were standing up in the deep wells of their sturdy boats, shifting their weapons to catch the sun.

Tannhahorens did not look at Mercy. The tip of his knife advanced and the Frenchman backed away from it. He was a very strong man, possibly stronger than Tannhahorens. But behind Tannhahorens were twenty heavily armed braves.

The Frenchman kept backing and Tannhahorens kept pressing. No sailor dared move a muscle, not outnumbered as they were. The Sauk let out a hideous wailing war cry.

Mercy shuddered with the memory of other war cries.

Even more terrified, all the French took another step back—and three of them fell into the St. Lawrence River.

The Sauk burst into wild laughter. The *voyageurs* hooted and booed. The sailors threw ropes to their floundering comrades, because only Indians knew how to swim.

Tannhahorens took Mercy's hand and led her to one of the pirogues, and the Sauk paddled close, hanging on to the edge of the dock so that Mercy could climb in.

Mercy could not look at the Sauk. She had shamed Tannhahorens in front of them.

Mercy climbed in and Tannhahorens stepped in after her, and the men paddled slowly upstream to Tannhahorens's canoe. The other pirogue stayed at the wharf, where those Sauk continued to stand, their weapons shining.

Eventually the French began to load the ship again.

"Daughter," said Tannhahorens, "the sailors are not good men."

She nodded.

He bent until he could look directly into her eyes, something Indians did not care for as a rule. "Daughter."

She flushed scarlet. On her white cheeks, guilt would always be revealed.

"The cross protects," said Tannhahorens. "Or so the French fathers claim. Perhaps it does. But better protection is to stay out of danger."

Did Tannhahorens think she had gotten lost? Did he believe that she had ended up on the wharf by accident? That she was waving the cross around for protection?

Or was he, in the way of Indians, allowing that to be the circumstance because it was easier?

When he had thanked the Sauk sufficiently and they had agreed to tell Otter that Mercy had gone home with her father, Tannhahorens paddled back to Kahnawake. His long strong arms bent into the current. Her family had not trusted her after all. Tannhahorens must have been following her.

Or, in the way of a real father, he had not trusted Montréal. Either way, she was defeated. There was no escape.

If there is no escape, and if there is also no ransom, what is there for me? thought Mercy. I don't want to be alone. A single star in a black and terrible night? How can I endure the name Alone Star? "Why do you call me Munnonock?" she asked.

She wanted desperately to go home and end this ugly day.

Home. It was still a word of warmth and comfort. Still a word of safety and love.

The homes she had known misted and blended and she did not really know if it was Nistenha in the long-house or Stepmama in Deerfield or her mother in heaven whose home she wanted.

"You are brave, daughter," said Tannhahorens without looking at her, without breaking his rhythm, "and can stand alone. You shine with courage, and so shone every night of your march. You are our hope for sons and daughters to come. On you much depends."

IN THE REMAINING WEEKS of autumn, they roasted chestnuts and gathered beechnuts, walnuts and butter-nuts. The girls shelled corn and dried apples and cran-berries. The boys shot pigeons and doves by the score, and geese migrating, and ducks. Bonfires never went out, and meat was constantly smoking.

Nistenha wove a basket of intricate design. She chose slender branches of willow, from which she had painstakingly scraped the thin yellow bark. Some she had soaked in butternut dye, and now, alternating wide and narrow bands, gold and brown, she created a complex pattern of light and dark. Then she sat Mercy in front of her, circling Mercy with her arms, and with her fingers ordered the movement of Mercy's.

It was exactly how her real mother had taught her to knit. Mercy closed her eyes and leaned back against Nistenha. What warmth and comfort there was within a mother's arms. Mercy began to weep. Mother, she prayed to her mother in heaven, please forgive me.

She blinked back her tears and only one splattered on the reeds in front of her. Together but separately, she and Nistenha finished the basket. It was a work of art.

"What is the occasion?" asked Mercy shakily. This basket had taken far too much time and care to be used for corn or laundry.

"Snow Walker will soon have a husband of her own," said Nistenha. "She must have fine gifts."

Mercy was delighted. "Great Angry Cloud?" she guessed happily.

"Of course. The families are pleased. It is good. Father Meriel will say the vows and write the names in his book."

Not the real names, though. Father Meriel would call Snow Walker by her French name, Jeanne. But what anybody's real name was, Mercy no longer knew. *You, Munnonock, are our hope for sons and daughters.*

Mercy's head spun. She made one last effort to push away the world of Kahnawake. "Nistenha. On that day when I went into Montréal . . . ?"

"Hush," said her mother. "We speak only of joyful things. Next I will show you how to etch a drawing on a birch-bark box you will make for Snow Walker."

She knows, thought Mercy. But in her world, you do not confess sins. You set them down.

"WE'RE GOING HUNTING," Joseph told Mercy at the end of the month. "Deer are gathering because it's rutting season. They'll be in the oak forests, eating acorns on the ground, so they'll be easy to find. Our family always goes north between the Matawin River and the Black."

"Our family?" said Ruth. But she did not say it loudly or with heat. They could see by the blackened vines how quickly winter was approaching; they could feel it in the morning, tasting sharp frost in the air. Ruth too wanted enough food to last the winter.

Some warriors would be gone for the entire winter; others would return in shifts, bringing meat. Bear, moose, deer, beaver, raccoon, fox. Some for food, all for fur.

But the party searching for bear came back more quickly than they meant to.

It was the work of a warrior to enter the cave, jab the bear awake and tempt him, grumpy and stuporous, to come out where he could be shot. No fur was so warm, no meat so good, no claws better ornaments. Of course, one swipe of that great paw could break a man's jaw or rip off an arm, but that was why it was so admired and why the warrior who goaded the bear got the claws: such impressive risk.

Altogether, the hunting party lost three men in poor judgment of bears.

The paw that swiped Tannhahorens in the face was given to his widow. His funeral was in church and in Latin. How soft the Mass was. How hard and fierce Tannhahorens had been.

Mercy was not comforted. Tannhahorens was just dead and the Mass was just noise. She was relieved when the Indians left the church and walked to the Place of the Dead, where the powwow led another ceremony and they could all howl and beat their breasts.

On me much depends. O Lord, does that mean that I take care of Nistenha now? That one day my son will be named Tannhahorens?

Nistenha and Tannhahorens's mother and sisters blackened their faces with soot and chopped their hair off raw and ugly, to lose their looks and grace. Nistenha would not let Mercy cut her hair, but she agreed to blacken Mercy's face in the color of sorrow.

The mourners paraded for several hours, but when Mercy went to join them, Ruth screamed. "How can you grieve for that murderer, Mercy? Remember his barbarous cruelties!"

So had Uncle Nathaniel said—*you must remember*. So had Mr. Williams said—*you must remember*. And one of the people Mercy would always remember was Tannhahorens. "He saved me, Ruth," she said sadly. "I owed him."

Ruth hauled Mercy down to the river. She threw the younger girl into the water and waded right in after her. The first crust of ice had formed and it splintered around their legs. Mercy could have fought back, but fighting was unthinkable because Ruth was right. A bear had avenged the Carter family, while Mercy had not.

Ruth scrubbed Mercy with sand, as if adopting her; as if washing away bad white blood. When Mercy's face was clean of soot and Ruth's rage spent, the girls climbed out of the water.

In Kahnawake everything was in the open. There was no cover, no place to hide. Soaked and shivering in the wind, she walked alone to her longhouse.

Nistenha left the mourners and came after her to wrap Mercy in blankets.

"Do you truly mourn your father?" asked Nistenha. How awful Nistenha looked, her face black and dripping, her hair jagged and torn, her clothing rent, her hands grimy from touching her sooty face.

Mercy nodded. She mourned all the fathers, English and Indian. She could not count as high as the number of fathers there were.

"Then I will give you just a little paint, one stroke on each cheek, to show how your heart hurts."

Mercy raised her face to accept the paint. "What about Ruth?"

"Do not worry," said Nistenha.

What capacity the Indians had not to worry. In Deerfield, all had been worry. Worry about the Lord, worry about sin. Worry about today, worry about tomorrow. Worry about crops, worry about children.

But Indians set worry down.

The next day, Mercy didn't see Ruth once, nor the day after that, nor the third day. Finally she sought out Otter. "Is Spukumenen ill?" said Mercy anxiously.

"She has been sold," said Otter. "She is in Montréal with the French nuns."

Mercy was astonished.

He had sold Ruth? This man who had accepted everything Ruth had ever done—from throwing packs to kicking him in the shins? From wearing French clothing to refusing to speak a syllable of Mohawk?

"When she could not let you mourn your father, it was best for her to go," said Otter.

Mercy wanted to sob. Difficult as Ruth was, Mercy would miss her terribly. She was Mercy's only enduring link to Deerfield. "Would you tell me why you gave her a second name, Otter? Let the Sky In?"

"She never told you? I am not surprised. She looked two ways on this. Once on the march, she and I stood at the edge of an ice cliff and it was I who lost our argument. I fell over and was much damaged. Ruth risked her life to save me," he said, using the English name Ruth had refused to surrender. "Without her, I would not again have seen the sky. But she was not glad to have done it. It was punishment for her to give me life."

Ruth had saved the life of her father's killer?

Oh, poor Ruth! Carrying her good deed with her! Knowing it was equally a bad deed!

Otter rested a hand on Mercy's shoulder. "Your Ruth is well. She will not miss us. We will miss her, for she did bring our sky in. Someday in Montréal, you will see her again. Now go with the children and play. You have mourned enough."

Chapter Twelve

The day of the adoption was cool and windy, with a gray sky and the ground wet from spring rains.

Mercy was trembling. *O Lord*, she prayed, and as in every prayer for a year and a month, she stopped there. She did not know what she was praying for, only that the presence of God was necessary. She prayed that He would know where to be and what to do.

It began to rain softly and lightly. Like a baptism, thought Mercy. The Lord himself supplies the water.

In the canoe, she was surrounded by Nistenha's family, but she hardly saw them and did not think of them. What would it be like to see an English child adopted? How would she feel, in her heart and in her soul, as the white blood was scrubbed out so that Indian blood ran true and forever?

She wondered if the boy wanted to be adopted. Not

that it mattered. There was no choice involved. The boy would make no promises and supply no answers. It was a magical cleansing, followed by a magical welcome. And she, and all other white captives, would be part of it: witnesses to the surrender of English blood.

The captives did not know the boy's name, because on such a day, the English name would not be spoken. They did not know if they would be allowed to talk to him or whether he came from Deerfield or from another of the many towns on the Maine or Massachusetts or New York frontiers. They did not know if he was three years old, like Daniel; almost a man, like Eben; or fourteen, like Joseph. Joseph and Mercy had both had birthdays since their capture.

I am twelve now, thought Mercy. Close to being a woman. I am treated as Nistenha's daughter. But she has never spoken of adopting me. I am still the child of Samuel Carter and his wife Mercy Brooks, sister of Nathaniel. I am still a child of Deerfield, Massachusetts.

She ordered herself to show courage during this adoption. Courage for the boy's sake, she wondered, or for mine? Carefully Mercy said, "Does the boy have a name given by his priest?" Sometimes the English name could be guessed from the French.

"Jean," said her uncle.

Heartbreak hit Mercy. *Jean* was the French way of saying John.

It could not be her brother John, for he lived in

Montréal and everyone said he was happy becoming French. O John! thought Mercy. *Please, God, let it be so, that he is happy.*

John was a popular name among Deerfield boys. This could be John Catlin, Ruth's brother, who would be seventeen now. John Burt, Sally Burt's brother-in-law, who was about twenty. It could be Jonathan Hoyt, Sarah's older brother, or John Stebbins, Thankful's older brother. Or, far more likely, John Field, age four.

Little John Field's sister Mary sat in a canoe a hundred yards downriver from Mercy. Mercy was almost never permitted to speak to Mary Field. What if it was Mary's very own baby brother being adopted, whom none of them had seen in a whole year?

It's nobody we know, Mercy told herself. It's a stranger, entering a strange life for good.

Mercy wanted to pray that the boy John was ready, that it would be easy for him, that he would be calm. But Ruth and Mr. Williams would expect Mercy to pray for the opposite: that he would refuse the adoption; that he might even fight to escape it.

Perhaps it was only Mercy whose heart was flung about like a leaf in a storm, for the others were thinking mostly of the feast. Joanna said, "I hope their corn lasted longer than ours. I hope we have something to eat at the feast besides meat and fish."

Kahnawake had used up its corn supply weeks ago.

No one had gone hungry because game remained plentiful. But a diet of nothing but meat was exhausting.

It was a long journey to the Abenaki fort of St. Francis.

When they finally clambered onto the shore, Mercy didn't like St. Francis half so much as Kahnawake. It wasn't clean or well planned. Its buildings were not attractive. The fields were not orderly and had not been made ready last fall. Nor was she impressed by the housing given to the guests. In fact, she found the entire village slovenly and dirty.

Mercy heard these thoughts as if someone else had uttered them. Of all the amazing things she had said to herself in the last year and month, this was the most amazing. She had become loyal to Kahnawake.

During the march, when Mercy was finding the Mohawk language such a challenge and a pleasure to learn, Ruth had said to Eben, "I know why the powwow's magic is successful. The children arrive ready."

The ceremony took place at the edge of the St. Francis River, smaller than the St. Lawrence but still impressive. The spray of river against rock, of ice melt smashing into shore, leaped up to meet the rain. Sacraments must occur in the presence of water, under the sky and in the arms of the wind.

There was no Catholic priest. There were no French. Only the language of the people was spoken, and the powwow and the chief preceded each prayer and cry with the rocking refrain *Listen, listen, listen.*

Joanna tugged at Mercy's clothes. "Can you see yet?" she whispered. "Who is it? Is he from Deerfield?"

They were leading the boy forward. Mercy blinked away her tears and looked hard. "I don't recognize him," she said finally. "He looks about fourteen. Light red hair. Freckles. He's tall, but thin."

"Hungry thin?" worried Joanna.

"No. I think he hasn't got his growth yet. He looks to be in good health. He's handsomely made. He is not looking in our direction. He's holding himself very still. It isn't natural for him, the way it is for the Indians. He has to work at it."

"He's scared then, isn't he?" said Joanna. "I will pray for him."

In Mercy's mind, the Lord's Prayer formed, and she had the odd experience of feeling the words doubly: "Our Father" in English, *"Pater Noster"* in Latin.

But Joanna prayed in Mohawk.

Mercy climbed up out of the prayers, saying only to the Lord that she trusted Him; that He must be present for John. Then she listened. This tribe spoke Abenaki, not Mohawk, and she could follow little of it. But often at Mass, when Father Meriel spoke Latin, she could follow none of it. It was no less meaningful for that. The magic of the powwow's chants seeped through Mercy's soul.

When the prayers ended, the women of John's family scrubbed him in sand so clean and pale that they must have put it through sieves to remove mud and shells and impurities. They scoured him until his skin was raw, pushing him under the rough water to rinse off his whiteness. He tried to grab a lungful of air before they dunked him, but more than once he rose sputtering and gasping.

The watchers were smiling tenderly, as one smiles at a new baby or a newly married couple.

At last his mother and aunts and sisters hauled him to shore, where they painted his face and put new clothing, embroidered and heavily fringed, on his body. As every piece touched his new Indian skin, the people cheered.

They have forgiven him for being white, thought Mercy. But has he forgiven them for being red?

The rain came down harder. Most people lowered their faces or pulled up their blankets and cloaks for protection, but Mercy lifted her face into the rain, so it pounded on her closed eyes and matched the pounding of her heart.

O Ruth! she thought. O Mother. Father. God.

I have forgiven.

FROM THE RIVER they walked back to the town, and the boy was taken into the fire circle outside the powwow's longhouse. Here he was placed on the powwow's sacred albino furs. A dozen men, those who were now his relatives, sat in a circle around him. The powwow lit a sacred pipe and passed it, and for the first time in his life, the boy smoked.

Don't cough, Mercy prayed for him. Don't choke.

Afterward she found out they diluted the tobacco with dried sumac leaves to make sure he wouldn't cough on his first pull.

Although the women had adopted him, it was the men who filed by to bring gifts. The new Indian son received a tomahawk, knives, a fine bow, a pot of vermilion paint, a beautiful black-and-white-striped pouch made from a skunk and several necklaces.

"Watch, watch!" whispered Snow Walker, riveted. "This is his father. Look what his father gives him!"

The warrior transferred from his own body to his son's a wampum belt—hundreds of tiny shell circles linked together like white lace. The belt was so large it had to hang from the neck instead of the waist.

To give a man a belt was old-fashioned. Wampum had no value to the French and had not been used as money by the Indians for many years. But it still spoke of power and honor and even Mercy caught her breath to see it on a white boy's body.

But of course, he was not white any longer.

"My son," said the powwow, "now you are flesh of our flesh and bone of our bone."

At last his real name was called aloud, and the name was plain: Annisquam, which just meant "Hilltop." Perhaps they had caught him at the summit of a mountain. Or considering the honor of the wampum belt, perhaps he kept his eyes on the horizon and was a future leader. Or like Ruth, he might have done some great deed that would be told in story that evening.

When the gifts and embraces were over, Annisquam was taken into the powwow's longhouse to sit alone. He would stay there for many hours and would not be brought out until well into the dancing and feasting in the evening.

Not one of Mercy's questions had been answered.

Was he, in his heart, adopted?

Had he, in his heart, accepted these new parents?

Where, in his heart, had he placed his English parents?

How did he excuse himself to his English God and his English dead?

The dancing began. Along with ancient percussion instruments that crackled and rattled, rasped and banged, the St. Francis Indians had French bells, whose clear chimes rang, and even a bugle, whose notes trumpeted across the river and over the trees.

"Mercy Carter!" exclaimed an English voice. "Joanna Kellogg! This is wonderful! I am so glad to see you!" An English boy flung his arms around the girls, embracing them joyfully, whirling them in circles.

Half his head was plucked and shiny bald, while long dark hair hung loose and tangled from the other half.

His skin was very tan and his eyes twinkling black. He wore no shirt, jacket or cape: he was Indian enough to ignore the cold that had settled in once the sun went down.

"Ebenezer Sheldon," cried Mercy. "I haven't seen you since the march."

He had been one of the first to receive an Indian name, when the snow thawed and the prisoners had had to wade through slush up to their ankles. Tannhahorens had changed Mercy's moccasins now and then, hanging the wet pair on his shoulder to dry. But Ebenezer's feet had frozen and he had lost some of his toes.

He hadn't complained; in fact, he had not mentioned it. When his master discovered the injury, Ebenezer was surrounded by Indians who admired his silence. The name Frozen Leg was an honor. In English, the name sounded crippled. But in an Indian tongue, it sounded strong.

The boys in Deerfield who were not named John had been named Ebenezer. That wouldn't happen in an Indian village. Each person must have a name exactly right for him; something that happened or that was; that reflected or appeared.

When Mercy and Joanna finished telling Frozen Leg everything that had happened to them in the past year, Mercy anxiously asked after Ebenezer's brother, Remembrance. She had heard nothing of his fate. It might be too terrible to be spoken of.

"We're both in Lorette," said Ebenezer cheerfully. "His family didn't come to this feast, though. Neither did Eben's. You know what is happening with Eben, don't you?"

"Will he marry Sarah?" Mercy asked excitedly. "We don't know how it worked out. Tell us."

"Father Meriel will honor Sarah's decision to accept Eben. I guess it's going to be quite an event. The French family does not accept Sarah's decision, and they're going ahead with their wedding plans. Eben's Indian family are going ahead with *their* wedding plans. There's going to be one bride, two grooms and a lot of armed men." Ebenezer was laughing about it. Mercy certainly hoped it was safe to laugh. "I don't think anybody will actually fight," said Ebenezer. "Father Meriel will straighten it out."

Mercy hadn't seen the priest in many weeks. She hoped he would visit Kahnawake soon. She missed him. "You must see my brother Sam every day."

He sighed and then he shrugged. "Yes. Go easy on him when you finally see him, Mercy. He's very Indian. I've never seen anybody take to hunting the way he has. In one year he's become an excellent shot. His family didn't come to this feast. I expect they'll adopt him and I expect they don't want him hearing arguments from you."

His family knows I am his sister, thought Mercy. They did not bring him here lest he talk to me.

"Your little brother Benny I haven't seen," Ebenezer Sheldon went on, "but Sam has run into him. Once when they went hunting, they stopped at Benny's village, which is quite a way south. Benny has forgotten all his English. Of course, he's only seven. A year is a long time when you're that little. As for your brother John, I've seen him twice in Montréal. He and Mary Brooks, your cousin, they're both Frenchified. She's Marie-Claire now and your brother's Jean. They love being French. I don't understand adoptions myself. I wouldn't want to be a father to somebody else's son. But the French and the Indians have run out of children. They love to pretend we're their children."

They aren't pretending, thought Mercy. Annisquam's mother and father were not pretending. Annisquam is their son.

"Do you know this boy Annisquam?" asked Joanna. "Where is he from?"

Ebenezer shook his head. "Nobody will say and he isn't allowed to talk to us. That doesn't surprise me. I'm usually separated from the other captives. We become Indian quicker if we don't have any English around us."

Joseph spoke up.

Mercy had almost forgotten that Joseph was along. Since his encounter with Mr. Williams, Joseph had been unwilling to talk about family. As soon as a captive referred to the past, Joseph melted away. Of all the captives, Mercy thought, Joseph suffered the most from wrestling with past and present.

"Have you become Indian?" said Joseph to Ebenezer.

Ebenezer made a disgusted face. "Absolutely not. I get along with them, but I do not permit a thought in my head to be Indian. It's different for me than it is for the three of you, though. Nobody in my Indian family attacked Deerfield. You and Mercy and Joanna deal with men who actually killed somebody in your family, but I'm just with Indians who bought me. It's easier. I promise you, Joseph, I'm going home one day. They could adopt me a hundred times and I'd still be English. So how's Kahnawake? I've never been there. Is it a trash heap like this?"

"Kahnawake is a beautiful town," said Mercy stiffly.

Ebenezer Sheldon laughed. "Watch your step, Mercy. They've got you by the ankle. Probably planning your adoption next."

Joseph looked away.

Joanna looked excited.

Lord, thought Mercy. *Lord, Lord, Lord.*

THEY STAYED in St. Francis for several days.

Mercy was careful not to be around Ebenezer Sheldon again, and careful not to examine the reasons why.

Minutes before the Kahnawake Indians stepped into

their canoes to paddle home, Mercy spotted the adopted boy walking alone. She darted between buildings to catch his arm. "Forgive me," she said in English. The language felt awkward and slippery, as though she might say the wrong thing. "I know you're not supposed to talk to us. But please. I need to know about your adoption."

Annisquam's look was friendly and his smile was pleasant. "You're one of the Deerfield captives, aren't you? I'm from Maine. Caught a few years before you."

She ached to know his English name, but he did not offer it. She must not dishonor whatever he had achieved. If he had become Indian, she must not encroach upon that. "Please, I need to know what happened when you were left alone inside the powwow's longhouse."

His freckles and his pale red hair were so unlikely above his Indian clothing. "Nothing happened. I just sat there."

Mercy was as disappointed as if he had forgotten his English. "I thought you would have been given answers." Her voice trembled. "Or been sure."

Annisquam looked at her for a long moment. "Nothing happened. But they *did* scrub away my past. I *was* born once more. I was one person when they pushed me under the water and another person when I left the powwow's. I'm not sure my white blood is gone. I will never forget my family in Maine. But I have set them down."

Mercy's head rocked with the size of that decision. *He set them down.* How had he done that? Every captive carried both: both worlds, both languages, both Gods, both families.

Listen, listen, listen, the powwows and the chieftains cried.

But so many voices spoke. How had Annisquam known which voice told the truth? How had he been sure what to set down and what to keep?

"But your parents," she said. "What would they think? Would they forgive you?"

His smile was lopsided and did not last long. "My parents," he said gently, "are waiting for me."

They stared at each other.

"Go with God," he whispered, and he walked away from her to join the man who had put the wampum belt around his neck and the woman who had washed him in the river.

Nistenha was teaching Mercy how to make bottles.

They separated birch-bark slabs into thin layers until they had a dozen flexible waterproof sheets. These pieces they sewed with European thread and needles. Mercy had a thimble that Otter had made for Ruth, which Ruth had flung into the fire and Snow Walker had rescued. It was a thimble with a lineage.

When Joseph swaggered up, Mercy knew from the way he walked that he was going to show off. She ignored him, taking another stitch.

"I feel so sorry for you, Munnonock," he said. "Sitting here squinting at a needle. I get to go west. You know what? We're going to be gone for a *year*. We're going to trade for furs. Great Sky says we paddle three oceans to get there."

The thimble fell from her finger and the needle followed it. *"A year?"*

"A year." Joseph was wild with excitement. "Annisquam and the Sheldon boys are coming too. Great Sky decided today, when Annisquam's father brought him here. We leave at dawn's first light to pick up the Sheldons and their fathers and we're off!"

How puzzling. Annisquam lived in St. Francis. Ebenezer and Remembrance Sheldon lived in Lorette. This was quite a party: men and boys from three towns. Men and boys who had not previously chosen to do anything together. All the boys white ... when white boys were generally kept separate from each other.

"Go paddle your rivers," said Nistenha, retrieving the precious needle before it vanished. "We will not miss you men, with your fighting and yelling and wrestling."

Joseph loved being referred to as a man. He had some of Nistenha's stew and told her how delicious it was.

Why was the group leaving so swiftly? Mercy wondered. Indian men rambled any time of the year, but they did not casually leave on major journeys. There were public prayers to be made, provisions to be set aside, wives to be considered. A year was a great length of time.

It was May. Last year, the men had stayed home during the summer, resting from a winter of danger and deprivation. For them it had been a richly deserved time of sun and ball games. Besides, hunting was difficult in summer, when the leaves of trees and the thick green of grass and shrubs could hide a deer only a few feet away.

She imagined Joseph leaping into the canoe, eager to do his share of the paddling and prove he was a man. What an adventure! And Joseph might be easier in his heart if he was far from Montréal, far from the stranger in the fields who was really his father.

Joseph had not called Great Sky Father since the day of Mr. Williams's visit, but just now he'd said "father" to refer to the men who would accompany Ebenezer and Remembrance and Annisquam.

"I will make a present for you, Sowangen," said Mercy. "Promise to wear it and remember me during your journey. A year is a long time."

But Joseph was already racing away, boasting to the boys who would be left behind.

Mercy and Nistenha worked long into the dark so her gift would be ready when the boys set out at first light. It would be his first tobacco pouch, a neck sash with pockets. She fringed the bottom edges and embroidered a row of tiny red and white beads. Joseph was too young for pipe and tobacco, but one day the warriors would let him smoke, and he must be ready.

She knew he would never set aside the tobacco sash, because he would be so pleased that Mercy saw him as a man.

When they had finished it, Nistenha got to her feet and stirred the stew, which did not need stirring, because everybody else had been asleep for hours, and were not about to eat. "You and I, Munnonock, as soon as the men have departed, will be looking for strawberries. My favorite field is many miles away. We will carry many baskets and plan to stay several nights."

Mercy did not look forward to that. Berries grew low to the ground, their leaves smothering and hiding the fruit. One basket of delicious sweet berries was worth a backache, but dozens of baskets? Mercy would be groaning with back pain every night. And the return trip home would be awkward and slow. Nistenha would choose two saplings, slicing away branches with a hatchet. She would walk first and Mercy second, and on their shoulders would rest the two poles, and from these would hang the heavy baskets. Mercy would also have to carry a burden pack to hold all the supplies.

Only yesterday, Nistenha had said she wanted a rest; she was tired from smoking so many fish; she was sick of work.

Mercy slept badly.

. . .

JOSEPH WAS THRILLED with his tobacco pouch, and Mercy thought that Great Sky was even more pleased.

Sadagaewadeh gave a quick prayer and a quicker speech.

The sun was only a faint pinkness and a touch of yellow in the east when two dugouts of French *voyageurs* pulled up to the jetty. Off they went: two canoes of Indians, two boats of French, paddles digging into the water like shovels into the earth, up the great river and out of sight.

For a year.

She could not comprehend it.

"We will leave shortly," Nistenha told Mercy. "While I prepare, I wish you to bake corn cakes. Plan for the two of us for a week. Snow Walker, you will do this with Munnonock."

When the girls arrived at the bake ovens, Mercy was aware of a general unease; a tension she did not usually feel among the Indians, and certainly not among women baking. There was little chatter. A surprising number of families were away. Aongote's family had left when it was still dark.

She and Snow Walker prepared a large tray of corn cakes and, as soon as they were done, beat the batter for a second batch.

There was a commotion at the jetty, but Mercy did not race to see who had arrived the way she used to. A horde of hungry children had surrounded her, and she was handing out cakes as fast as she could spread the maple butter. There was nothing more pleasurable than giving food to children. "You will have to start over," said Snow Walker. "They've eaten all but four cakes."

In Deerfield, there would have been much irritation that the same chore must be repeated the very same morning. But an Indian would not think of it that way: food was for eating and children were for joy.

Mercy turned back to see if the ovens were free so she could start her next batch, and her eyes fell on the activity at the jetty. And then there was no turning back. Eight white men stood on the stones by the river.

Six French soldiers.

One Catholic priest.

And a Deerfield survivor, Deacon Sheldon, whose sons had left at dawn to be away for a year.

The woven reed tray slipped from Mercy's fingers and dropped lightly to the ground. The four remaining corn cakes scattered and the dogs pounced on them.

Ransom had arrived.

"STAY HERE," said Snow Walker frantically. "You must stay here."

"No," said Mercy courteously, although Mohawk had no word for "no" and the closest she could come was *jaghte oghte.* Maybe not.

Snow Walker caught Mercy's wrist, but Mercy looked

at her sharply and Snow Walker let go. Among Indians, your body was your own. Others could not interfere with it.

"No, Munnonock," whispered Snow Walker. "Please. Much depends on you."

Mercy walked around several Indian women who stood in her path, holding out their hands and silently beseeching. Had Nistenha planned better, she and Mercy would have been miles away among the strawberries, and Mercy would never have known who had arrived in Montréal.

Joseph would never know. Ebenezer and Remembrance Sheldon would never know. Eunice Williams, Aongote, would never know.

Gathering on the jetty were several Indian families, her own included. Tannahorens's mother and sisters. Snow Walker's mother. Nistenha's mother. Otter and Ruth's former family. Joanna's. Aongote's distant relatives. Joseph's mother's family.

Sadagaewadeh wore necklaces, his neck pouch with its sacred talisman and his silver cross. The priest was one who substituted for Father Meriel, and the English deacon—*oh, the deacon!*

Mercy floated on waves of memory.

Deacon Sheldon had built a great new house the year before the attack. Its second floor overhung the first, making it easier to defend, because it was safer to shoot from those upper windows. His house hadn't saved anybody. She remembered seeing the Indians hack at the huge oak door whose hinges Deacon Sheldon had been so proud of: heavy cast-iron hinges and bolt. Mistress Sheldon had been shot right through the hole in the door—Ebenezer and Remembrance had seen it happen.

Tannhahorens, thought Mercy dizzily. *He Splits the Door.* But it can't have been that door; he already possessed that name.

She thought of the Deerfield captives Mr. Sheldon would try to ransom. There must be dozens still alive. Of the adults, Mercy had seen only Mr. Williams; not once had she laid eyes on another Deerfield parent.

Who, thought Mercy, will return with Deacon Sheldon? My brothers? Perhaps Deacon Sheldon has already ransomed them. Perhaps even now they are on an English ship, ready to sail for an English port. Boston. Massachusetts. Home.

And Eben and Sarah? Would his Indian family, having taken on the French so that Eben could have his bride, now shrug and let them sail away?

Sally and Benjamin Burt? Would their families surrender not only the couple, but also baby Christopher, whom every Indian girl took turns cuddling?

The de Fleury family, who had turned Cousin Mary into Marie-Claire—they spent more money on Marie-Claire's clothing than Massachusetts would raise for all the ransoms. Would they hand their daughter over to Deacon Sheldon?

Joanna was still in Kahnawake, unless they had taken her with Aongote. Joanna, whose prayers were in Mohawk. Would her family surrender her? Rebecca, the other Kellogg sister, had moved away with her Indian family months ago.

And Aongote. Little Eunice Williams. Mr. Sheldon would try to get the Williams family home first, because the minister was related to such important people. But Aongote was important to her Indian family, and her strong name—Planted—would work against any removal.

Ruth! She must be wild with excitement. All over again Mercy saw Ruth throwing Joanna's pack into the snow—the fry pan and the leg of lamb and the knife flying all over the place.

Nistenha tied a scarf over Mercy's hair.

Mercy took it off.

Snow Walker stepped in front of Mercy.

Mercy circled her and went on. She was at the end of another journey. The world beyond ransom seemed as unknown as Kahnawake had one year ago.

Nistenha blocked Mercy's path. All these months, she had remained blackened and torn in widowhood. She did not touch Mercy but wrapped her arms around her own body and hugged herself. "Daughter," she said to Mercy, but no sound came out. It was just the motion of dry lips. Their eyes met and Mercy thought, Who is this woman?

"She suffers," whispered Snow Walker, and Mercy thought, So do I.

From the jetty, the highest-ranking French officer spoke first. "My people," he said in Mohawk, "this man comes from the town of Deerfield, much known to you in war. He offers much money if you give their sons and daughters back. I am honor bound to tell you that those who still live in Deerfield miss their children and are in much pain at their loss. The parents of Deerfield beg your forgiveness. The mothers and fathers of Deerfield pray for your understanding. They ask for their children."

No parent in Deerfield would ever ask forgiveness from an Indian. Forgiveness? they would demand. For what?

But it was nicely said. Mercy admired a translator who knew better than to translate.

Tannhahorens's mother joined Nistenha, holding up a hat of soft plain deerskin for Mercy to wear. It had no fringe, no dangling foxtail. It was a covering to hide Mercy's yellow English hair.

The priest said, "If it is in your heart to return a child whom you yourself have come to love, the ransom money shall be yours. But remember, the English are not Catholic. Your sons and daughters will be lost to hell if they are returned."

The men were trained to speak loudly: the officers so

their voices would carry over wind and water, battle and gunshot; the priest so his voice would rise to God.

Mercy stood inside a tight circle of older, heavier, taller women. She did not try to push through. When she was ready, she would call out. Her hair and eyes would be her proof.

"How many Deerfield children are actually in Kahnewake?" demanded Mr. Sheldon. He of course spoke English, and that had to be translated both for the soldiers and for the priest, because Father Meriel alone was fluent in English.

"We think there are about fifteen," said the priest finally, "but it is difficult to be sure. The Indians move them around, and of course the Indians themselves move quite a bit. Soon many will go to summer camps, where the fishing is better. They are not an easy people to count."

"And my sons?" said Mr. Sheldon. "My children? Where are my sons? Remembrance and Ebenezer?"

"They've gone hunting," said Sadagaewadeh.

Slowly, ready to be knocked aside, Tannhahorens's mother lowered the hat over Mercy's head. How soft the skin was, beaten for so many hours.

"When will my sons return? When do I see them?" Mr. Sheldon's voice betrayed fury that a savage dared make the rules for a deacon from Massachusetts.

"They've gone hunting," said Sadagaewadeh again.

Indians did not like the English habit of going over and over something.

There was silence, with which Indians were comfortable and English were not.

Nistenha wept. Tears ran through the soot she still applied in honor of Tannhahorens, leaving streams of sorrow on her cheeks.

Mr. Sheldon shouted, "Where are my sons?"

Nobody spoke.

Even Mercy, who could have told him, did not speak.

Listen, listen, listen, came so many voices: every adult of her first childhood and every adult of her second world.

For the first time since her capture, Mercy saw Deerfield clearly, and all her relations and neighbors and friends. She saw the hills bright in autumn and heard the laughter of children coming from school, the snap of an English flag in the wind. She saw the grave of her birth mother, and she almost saw the newer graves next to it, those who had died on a snowy morning in 1704.

Deacon Sheldon's voice broke. "Please! I have lost my children. Surely you know how terrible that is. Permit me at least to speak to them."

Go forward, Mercy told herself. He cannot speak to his sons, for they have been removed, but I can tell him what he needs to know. He will lift me in his arms, crying, "Mercy! Mercy Carter!" He will turn my face up like an offering and thank the Lord that I who was lost am found.

But am I lost?

And am I Mercy Carter?

I will remember, she had promised Uncle Nathaniel. I will remember my family, my God and my home.

I have not broken my promise. I remember my family with love. I honor my God in every way . . . and in every language. And my home—*oh, my home.*

Is it here?

It seemed to Mercy that she needed more time—weeks, months, even years—to know the answer to that question. She had been thinking about it since May of 1704, and yet she did not know. Annisquam had set it down. Mercy carried it all, the burden strap of memory still cutting her forehead.

The French priest asked the deacon if he would like to enter the French church and see where the children of Deerfield worshiped, but Deacon Sheldon shook his head in horror and walked back to the boat.

Mercy Carter closed her eyes. *Lord, Lord, Lord.*

Latin slipped into her prayer, and Mohawk, and French, and she felt herself swept away by so many languages. So many fears and hopes were the same, so many answers as hard to find, in every language.

When she finished speaking to the Lord, Deacon Sheldon was gone.

And so was Mercy Carter.

THE GIRL who had been Mercy Carter stood for a long time watching the canoes disappear down the St.

Lawrence. She had waved after Daniel, had been too crushed to wave after Sarah and Eben, and never thought of waving after Deacon Sheldon.

Ransom, she thought. I didn't take it.

Nistenha removed the hat, folded it and touched the heavy gold braids. "Daughter?"

It seemed to the girl that sky and wind and river held their peace and waited to hear. Mother, she thought, beloved mother in heaven, forgive me. I walk now into another life. "Nistenha," she said.

"It is your choice? For if not, my daughter, we follow them."

I follow where the world took me. Mother. Father. Love me anyhow. I shall always love you.

"It is my choice," said Nistenha's daughter.

The Endings

OF THE 109 PRISONERS taken from Deerfield, 88 survived the march; 59 eventually returned to Massachusetts; 29 stayed behind, every one less than twenty years old.

Mercy Carter married a Kahnawake Indian.

Her brother Ebenezer (Benny in this story) was ransomed in 1706.

Her brother Samuel remained Indian but did not live much longer. He drowned in the St. Lawrence River.

Her brother John became Jean Chartier and married Marie Courtemanche. They had eleven children.

Ruth Catlin was ransomed in 1707.

Eben Nims and his bride, Sarah Hoyt, were not ransomed until 1714.

Mr. Williams was ransomed, but not his daughter Eunice, who stayed with the Mohawks and married an Indian named Arosen—Squirrel.

Sally and Benjamin Burt had a second child on the voyage home after their ransom. The child was named Seaborn.

Joseph Kellogg stayed with both French and Indians for several years. In 1710 he may have been the first New Englander to reach the Mississippi River. He did not come home to Massachusetts until 1716, and for many years was the Indian interpreter for army forts on the frontier.

Joanna Kellogg married an Indian. So did her sister Rebecca.

Eliza, widow of the Indian Andrew Stevens, married a Frenchman and stayed in Canada.

Nobody ever knew what happened to Daniel.

Author's Note

WHEN I WAS IN ELEMENTARY SCHOOL, I loved three books about Indian captives: *Sword of the Wilderness* by Elizabeth Coatsworth (who was a Newbery Award winner for another book), *Indian Captive*, a Newbery Honor Book by Lois Lenski, and *Black River Captive* by West Lathrop. I loved reading about the frontier, the settlers and the Indians. My children have a far-back grandmother from Massachusetts, an Indian named Welcome Mason. My nephew Ransom is descended from John Gillett, mentioned briefly in this book. He is named according to a family tradition in honor of the ransom paid to get John Gillett home.

Once when I was driving through Deerfield, I decided to research John Gillett. I got swept up in the story of 1704 instead.

John Williams, the minister, wrote a memoir: *The*

Redeemed Captive Returning to Zion. He told how Eunice was given rides on a sled and how many moccasins were provided. He was rough on his own captured children as they slid into being Catholic, and he wrote brutal letters to them. He did see Eunice eventually, but she never accepted ransom.

His son Stephen (whom I don't mention in my story) was taken to Canada by a different route, and he also wrote a brief memoir.

There are family legends: that Ruth Catlin threw her pack at the Indians; that Eben Nims rescued Sarah Hoyt from marriage to a Frenchman.

There are objects: A prisoner leash, of the kind worn by Nathaniel Brooks, is on display in the Deerfield Museum, as is an Indian sash brought back by Stephen Williams.

There are official records in Boston, Montréal and Deerfield. Father Meriel, very unusual in his ability to speak English, recorded births, baptisms, marriages and deaths. These were researched a hundred years ago by Emma Coleman of Deerfield, who found out what happened to almost every captive from New England.

I used real Indian names where I could, although few are certain. Thorakwaneken is actually the name of a grandson of Eunice Williams. Gassinontie, Flying Legs, was her daughter. Tannhahorens was the owner of Mr. Williams, rather than Mercy, but his name does mean "He Splits the Door." Aongote was the name given to

Eunice and does mean "Planted." New England Indian vocabulary is poorly known, because language as it was spoken in 1704 has vanished. In early accounts, the spelling of Mercy's Indian town is Caughnawaga; today historians prefer Kahnawake.

I chose Mercy Carter to write about because I wanted to make Mercy up, and we don't know much except the names and birth dates of her family. I wanted to write about somebody who refused to be ransomed home.

Her real father was still alive. Having lost his entire family in 1704, Samuel Carter moved to Connecticut. When he died in 1728, his will left a large sum to Mercy if she and her Indian family would come to live there, but they never did. So he knew she was alive and hoped for her return.

Mercy's brother Ebenezer (I call him Benny in this story to distinguish him from the other Ebenezers) accepted ransom and also moved to Connecticut. In 1751 two of Mercy's half-Indian sons visited their uncle Ebenezer. So Mercy had not forgotten who she was, and had told her children, and somehow kept up with her redeemed brother and lonely father. Did letters go back and forth between them? If so, those letters don't exist now.

But this we know: she chose not to be English again.

Deacon Sheldon and other Deerfielders came to Canada year after year, searching for captives and bringing some home each time. But even after the

French government agreed that every prisoner could go home (when the French and Indian war called Queen Anne's War ended) some captives still refused. It does not appear that the Indians used force or deceit to keep them.

Some captives even said no to their own families. Joseph Kellogg, redeemed in 1713, went back to French Canada in 1718 to coax his sisters Rebecca and Joanna to come home with him. They refused. He tried again ten years later, and Rebecca did return, but Joanna still refused.

Many Indians who had to give up their adopted children later came to visit them in Deerfield. It is amazing to imagine these Indians arriving in the town they once burned, now camping in the fields and attending church with adults who once lived with them as children. Indians visited the Sheldons in Deerfield so often that the Sheldon family asked Boston to help pay the expense of feeding them.

So there was deep affection between these Indian families and their white children. There was love. Still, Mercy must have loved her birth family. Why wasn't that love stronger? Shouldn't she have chosen to return to them? How could she have preferred to stay with people who more or less kidnapped her?

This is the question every English colonist had. Why and how did captive English children so readily become Indians? Benjamin Franklin wrote that Indians have a "life of ease, of freedom from care and labor ... all wants supplied by nature." Indians visit Boston, he added, and "see no reason to change. Going Rambling is so much more fun." Ben Franklin wondered which life was better—an Indian's or a settler's—and answered himself, "Too much care and pain is necessary to support our type of life."

But would Mercy stay in a different land with a different language, a different religion, a very different way of life—*and different parents!*—just to have fewer chores?

I believe Mercy chose to stay in Kahnawake because of love.